Wylder Hearts

by

Kim Turner

The Wylder West

Wylder Hearts

Cover Art by *Tina Lynn Stout*

The Wild Rose Press, Inc.
PO Box 708
Adams Basin, NY 14410-0708
Visit us at www.thewildrosepress.com

Publishing History
First Cactus Rose Edition, 2020
Trade Paperback ISBN 978-1-5092-3468-4
Digital ISBN 978-1-5092-3469-1

The Wylder West
Published in the United States of America

The businessman bolted forward and swung a fist that made contact with his chin, leaving him off balance and staggering backward. Trying to avoid the crowd that had collected, he bobbled and went down, expecting to hit the ground. But the impact never came. Instead he landed softly to a shrill feminine scream, and the greenest eyes he'd ever beheld.

Time simply froze, the world around him a haze as he found himself mesmerized by the beauty of the woman beneath him. It had been a damn long time since he was in such a position as this.

Unable to move with the crowd about them, he apologized, allowing a slight smile to curl his lips, though he knew he should get back to the fight. He reached to tip his hat and realized he'd lost it. The feel of her bosom pressed between them stirred up a thing or two. "Beggin' your pardon, ma'am."

"I'm quite all right." She pushed to rise, but the crowd surrounding them was thick.

"Actually, I was apologizing for this." Caleb bent to kiss her, slow and searing, her lips plump and tender, holding him there a moment longer than needed. He held her surprised green-eyed gaze a moment more and then he was back to the fight.

Dedication

For the mustangs,
who should be left to the untouched wilds…

Chapter One

The heat of the afternoon hung heavy as Caleb Holt tied his horse, Jericho, to the hitching post outside the Wylder Feed & Seed. He leaned against the building, focusing on the corral behind the livery. The town was busy enough, as usual, but it was time he did what needed doing. He didn't expect things to go too well as he stepped forward.

As suspected, the red bay he'd sold last week to Tucker Johnson was still the brunt of the man's anger, something his uncle Russ Holt had let him know from a recent jaunt to town. Horses from the Holt ranch weren't sold to be beaten and abused. Seems Johnson wasn't happy with the feisty temperament of the horse he'd purchased from Caleb and had lifted a crop to her. Worse yet was Chet Daniels, who ran the livery, had done nothing about it. Well, he damn well knew better than to allow the man to harass one of his horses.

He nodded, adjusting his hat and looking on from a distance as Johnson used a crop to try and calm the red bay. Hell, the horse was spirited but never in distress. It was clear Johnson, a traveling salesman, knew little about the animal. And he'd been warned.

He studied the men around the corral watching Johnson yield the crop as if the scene was something out of a circus. He sucked in a deep breath, forcing his pulse to calm. He only sold his horses to men who would do them right and treat them with the respect such animals deserved. He was here to take the bay back, which wouldn't be to Johnson's liking. The man with gold-lined pockets flashed his money around town a little too easily, and Caleb scolded himself for ever thinking he would do right by the horse.

Caleb walked with purpose toward the livery, the weight of his revolver touching low on his left hip, but he needed no gun for what he was about to do. His reputation was well-known around town and as he stopped at the corral, some of the men at the fencing backed off. A few moved to the opposite site. They all knew why he'd come. Johnson was about to know it, too. He'd never raised a whip or crop to any of his animals but he might just put it across the salesman's back given the chance.

Johnson continued gripping the rope tied to the mare, trying to have the bay run a circle but the horse wasn't cooperating, agitated, her tail high and her ears perked in alarm.

Caleb glanced across the corral as Chet Daniels came from inside the livery, holding his knowing gaze. He expected the man to have handled this before now. A hush fell as Caleb lifted the rope off the gate and stepped into the corral, waiting as Johnson turned, the chubby man's face red with the work at hand.

"Interesting thing about horses, Johnson. Most react appropriately to how they are treated, much like a woman." Caleb held his voice steady. "Though I'll reckon you know little about either."

Some of the men around the corral chuckled in echo.

"I've not harmed the horse, she just needs a little

training to let her know who's boss." The fancy-dressed man postured, his business suit dusty and damp with perspiration. Johnson was a jewel merchant, a man who moved town to town, paying for gold and selling stones most often to those he swindled out of their money.

Caleb eased closer to the anxious mare and placed a hand to her side and moved his other hand across her, the horse calming and easing toward him. "Easy, girl. That's it."

She was aware she was safe for the moment, at least with him.

"I'll be damned," a cowboy whispered along the fencing.

"The man knows horses for sure. Ain't nothing good gonna come out of this. He'll kick Johnson's ass for this one sure 'nough." Another's whisper faded as a hush fell across the corral again.

Caleb eased his palm against the animal once more. "Easy, girl...easy. It's all right, gonna take you back home."

Johnson stepped closer. "You're taking her nowhere, Holt. I paid for this one and will treat her how I see fit."

The bay startled at the man's tone, though Caleb stayed with her, keeping eye contact. He lifted the lead clipped to her halter and began to tug her toward the gate he'd come through. It was time to take her home, give her a rest and a bit of care and then see about selling her in Colorado or elsewhere.

"She's mine, damnit!" Johnson shouted, following, his fists balled as he huffed and puffed to catch up.

Caleb turned, holding the man's dark-eyed gaze. He reached into his trouser pocket and dropped a handful of rolled bills to the ground at Johnson's feet. "You lost that right when you raised a crop to her."

Tucker cursed, scrambling to pick up the paper money that began moving with the wind. "You bastard, I'll have my animal back. You hear me, Holt, you hear me?"

Caleb heard the man but led the bay back toward Jericho. Untying his mount, he led both horses away on foot, not wanting to startle the horse any further as they made their way through town. It wasn't the first time he'd taken a horse back and it wouldn't be the last. Holt Ranch had a reputation to uphold, where good horses were raised, broken, and sold, not a one ever knowing evidence of a crop or other abuse. His father's legacy was to be respected.

He always gave clear instructions when he sold a horse and Johnson had crossed that line. Maybe he'd never heard the Holt name until now. Well, that was the man's second mistake.

He glanced at the Five Star Saloon, which stayed full of patrons most all day and night. He couldn't be certain his uncle Russ wasn't inside having himself another rotgut afternoon. That or he might be found at the Wylder Social Club, spending time with the local madam, Miss Adelaide. He shook his head. Uncle Russ hadn't been home this morning, no doubt he was in one place or the other.

Well, he'd pass on the liquor, as he wasn't much of a drinking man when it came down to it anyway. He turned back to the road, an odd sound reaching his ears a split second before his senses kicked in. Coldcocked across his back. Tucker Johnson was the one levying a fist. Both horses reared and escaped Caleb's grasp. As he turned, a fist found his cheek. *Son of a bitch!*

Before Tucker caught him again, Caleb swung and the man's head popped back with the blow. "Look, Johnson, you don't want this fight, now back off."

"That's my animal, paid for in full, Holt." Johnson hit him again, and the impact sent him flying backward. The man was twice his size but altogether clumsy about it.

"I'll be teaching you the same respect as the horse." Johnson swung and missed as Caleb dodged him. He was lighter on his feet. The city slicker wasn't a fighter. One good punch and Caleb could lay him out on the street. His father and uncle had taught him to fight, and it wouldn't take much to make things bad for Johnson.

"You're not deserving of one of my animals, should've never trusted you would be." Caleb planted another punch across the man's brow for effect. "Back off if you don't want a fight, Johnson, because you definitely don't want this one."

The businessman bolted forward and swung a fist that made contact with Caleb's chin, leaving him off balance and staggering backward. Trying to avoid the crowd that had collected, he bobbled and went down, expecting to hit the ground. But the impact never came. Instead he landed softly to a shrill feminine scream, and the greenest eyes he'd ever beheld.

Time simply froze, the world around him a haze as he found himself mesmerized by the beauty of the woman beneath him. It had been a damn long time since he was in such a position as this.

Unable to move with the crowd about them, he apologized, allowing a slight smile to curl his lips, though he knew he should get back to the fight. He reached to tip his hat and realized he'd lost it. The feel of her bosom pressed between them stirred up a thing or two. Beggin' your pardon, ma'am."

"I'm quite all right." She pushed to rise, but the crowd surrounding them was thick.

"Actually, I was apologizing for this." Caleb bent to kiss her, slow and searing, her lips plump and tender, holding him there a moment longer than needed. He held her surprised green-eyed gaze a moment more and then he was back to the fight.

Johnson swung a fist and then another, though Caleb avoided the blows, waiting for a chance to land a solid left hook to Johnson's chin, and caught him hard. The man held his gaze for a single second before his eyes rolled back and he fell to the ground.

Caleb cursed under his breath and grabbed the knuckles of his left hand with his right. "Shit! I tried to warn you." Most of the town knew he could fight, and that he didn't care much for it.

He turned to find the woman. She was no longer there behind him, the crowd having swallowed her up. Damn. He grabbed his hat from the ground, dusted it and slapped it on his head as Chet Daniels handed him the leads to the horses once more.

"Sorry, Holt, didn't know what Johnson had in mind about the bay." The man tried to make excuses, but little happened at the livery that Daniels didn't know about.

"I think we both should've." Caleb turned and continued his jaunt through town, mounting up just outside of the Wylder Social Club and turning back once more, wondering about the woman he'd kissed.

He shook his head. It had been rather rude of him but he'd never seen eyes as green as hers and he'd never tasted anything so sweet. Best he hit the trail home before some husband came looking for him. He couldn't have ever seen her before, he would've remembered eyes that color. He wasn't even sure what had caused him to kiss her like that right in front of the entire town. He placed a finger to his upper lip where it still tingled, wondering if that had come from a punch or the tenderness of that kiss he'd taken without permission. She'd been a real beauty and as it was, he was sure he'd be back to town real soon to see just who owned that set of eyes the deep color of a forest.

****

The afternoon heat filled the sewing room enough to make the windows steam, that or the hot wash water just outside the window fogged the thin glass. Laurel ran an arm across her brow, wiping the sweat from her forehead, and rocked the pedal on her mother's sewing machine. She lined a solid stitch down the seam of a cotton skirt, much like the one she wore.

Behind her, Jesse grew restless, the few toys he had there were not enough to occupy him for long these days. He leaned against her side, whining to be held, though it was a little past his time to nap.

"It's all right, go play, Mama won't be too much longer." Laurel whispered, though she reached down to run a hand across the light brown locks sticking to his forehead.

Across the room at the counter, the Widow Lowery, the elderly woman who owned the Lowery Dress Shoppe, handed off a bundle of clothing to one of the women from town. The dress shop stayed busy most

7

days. She turned as the woman left, took in clothing from another and tossed the linen out the back door, where Leona Fabray, the wash woman, kept hot boiling pots going most all day long.

"Miss Fabray, we'll need this bag washed by tomorrow. I suggest you get to it this afternoon so it's got time to dry by mornin'." The widow let the door slam behind her as Leona protested that she already had several bags of clothing to go.

The widow fanned herself and shuffled Laurel's way. The heavy-set elderly woman had a tough time of the heat each day. "We'll need that last skirt tonight, Ms. Adams, best get the lad off to his toys. I told you, he's not gonna abide much with sitting idle now he's almost three."

"Yes, ma'am, he'll be fine and I'll have the skirt finished soon." Laurel handed a cookie from her bag to Jesse, who nabbed it and scampered off to his small play area, allowing her to focus once more on the skirt.

She was used to the widow being a bit testy with her and Leona, but it seemed the three of them got through the work days each week, getting everything accomplished. She glanced at the clothing hanging on a bar on the wall before her. It was lined with more work for next week, the skirt being the last of what she had to complete since today was Saturday.

She wiped her brow again and finished the hem, turning the skirt right side out again to inspect her work. Gunshots blasted from across the street. She jumped and Jesse began to cry and ran back to her once more.

"Those darn rowdies from the railroad." The widow moved to the doorway, mumbling under her breath as she grabbed the heavy broom that stayed there. "They come in here every afternoon and shoot their guns like it's quitting time for all of us, seems that no-good lazy sheriff Hanson would get after them, that or retire like he should. If it isn't them then some wild cowboys will be the ones blasting up the place to frighten us all to death."

Leona entered through the back door folding a large drying cloth. "Well, the town is called Wylder, guess it's a-livin' up to its name and the sheriff can't retire until he finds someone to replace him."

"Well, somethin' needs to be done about him, too, if'n he can't handle things around here anymore." The widow, who was more than efficient at using the broom to run men from the dress shop, set it aside. "Not to mention Mr. Holt knocking you down, dear." She glanced at Laurel.

Seemed everyone in town knew about that and— the kiss he'd stolen. She'd been embarrassed at the time, but now her lips tingled any time she thought of Caleb Holt.

She lifted Jesse to her knee. "Oh, it's all right, now." She cradled her son for a moment, the regular gunfire in and around town always startled him to tears. It wasn't like they had a day without some of it, though.

He sniffled and began chewing on his cookie once more, one small hand gripping tight to the front of her shirt as she continued to sew. She glanced at the widow, who had stepped back to her work on the other machine across the room, thankful she wasn't as demanding today. There were days she was quite overbearing and less tolerable when Jesse had a fussy day.

Laurel turned the skirt and began another seam. At

least the widow was most always pleased with her work, something she prided herself on. The fact she owned and knew how to work the sewing machine that had once belonged to her mother had helped land the job when she'd first arrived in town.

She wiped her brow once more with her forearm as Jesse settled against her and batted his eyes. It was time for his nap and if she continued her work, he'd fall asleep in no time. He was getting so big, his upcoming birthday a reminder another year had passed for them both.

She continued to work on the skirt, letting her mind drift. And it had been just as long since she'd arrived in Wylder, a town in the Wyoming Territory, south of the mining camp…the mining camp where she'd found herself abandoned by her husband, Jonah, Jesse's father.

It seemed like such a short time, though she still had no answers. She'd traveled west with her new husband four years before. He'd promised it wouldn't be long before he put a down payment on a homestead—something that had never happened. She'd lived her new marriage and her pregnancy in the tent at a mining camp, even delivering Jesse alone with no help of a doctor or midwife, the hardest thing she'd ever done in her twenty-two years.

She shouldn't have been surprised by any of it. She'd known Jonah's ways early on, but she'd believed his promises and somehow had been caught up in the excitement he'd one day make a strike—that never came either. And one day, he'd not returned to camp, having taken most of their money, and left her with their two-year-old son, the palomino she called Pink, her mother's sewing machine, and—a shattered heart.

She'd had little money, but in asking her first day in Wylder, she'd been pointed to Lowery's Dress Shoppe. It took the widow a second to look at her and deny her the job advertised in the window, but she'd begged for a chance to prove her work. That had changed the widow's mind the same day, and the elderly woman who was cranky most all the time, offered her the room upstairs and an old crib for Jesse as well.

There was no sense in playing it all through her mind once again. Jonah was gone and she'd made her way without him, doing her best not to look back, though she often wondered what had become of him. She supposed a broken heart wasn't easily mended, but it was still hard to fathom he'd up and left them with no word at all.

She shook off the thought. With today being Saturday, she would be able to spend tomorrow at the meadow by the creek outside of town. The best part of that was the time with her son and Pink, who without a doubt had become her best friend.

She glanced down at her small son, now sleeping against her breasts, the cookie still in his hand. He loved sticking his feet in the creek and running in the grass of the meadow. It was quiet there, warm in the sun and cool in the shade.

She supposed she'd be scolded by the widow again for not attending Sunday services at the local church, but it wasn't like she'd found any real welcome there. Most were more interested in the reasons her husband was no longer with her, so she'd settled to the fact that it was no one's business save her own, and she hadn't gone back.

"Don't know how you sew with that there machine so quickly, Laurel, not sure I could ever do something like that." Leona bit into an apple and chewed with her mouth open as she talked. The young woman worked very hard at the wash and had become one of the only friends Laurel had made in the busy town. She was young, near her same age and dressed in men's pants and shirts way too big for her. She kept her hair pulled up under a big floppy hat, never seeming to apply a brush.

Laurel shrugged, sorting a pile of threads. "I suppose I could sew in my sleep. My mother taught me on this very machine from an early age. I could teach you, if you like."

"I'm always mesmerized in watchin' how well ya' do it," Leona went on. "I've enough to do with that pile of dirty drawers and linens on the tables out back. My goodness, it's scorching hot in here, good thing we'll be done soon. Guess I better get out there again 'afore the widow takes a strap to me or something." She giggled, glancing behind her. "You a-goin' out to the creek again tomorrow?"

Laurel nodded. "I think so, it's usually nice for Jesse to play and Pink to run."

"Well, ya' be careful alone out there, these ruffians from town can be overbearing as you already know with Mr. Holt knocking you right down." Her friend shook her head. "But him giving you that kiss. He's probably the handsomest man this side of the muddy Mississippi, rich too, at least in horses and land." Leona lifted her brows, teasing as she hung at the door.

"Well, I hardly think the kiss was of real purpose."

Laurel glanced back to her sewing, wishing all would forget that kiss—including her.

"I don't know. I seen him a lot in town, never talks much to the ladies nor the whores in the social club but he sure had eyes for you." Leona said it matter of fact, grinned and then escaped back to her wash.

Laurel continued with her task. Mr. Holt was a handsome man, especially when she'd held his gaze for the brief second it had taken him to steal the kiss from her. She supposed given how a lot of men in town were way too forward, she should be more careful. But if Wylder had taught her anything, it was perseverance in how to protect herself. The fact she owned a small pistol was proof enough of that, though she wasn't sure how to use the darn thing.

Cock it, point, and shoot. Chet Daniels, the owner of the livery, had told her she'd need a gun if she was staying any time in Wylder, and had sold it to her at a fair price. He'd been very kind to her in promising to take care of Pink.

Her mind drifted to Mr. Holt once more. The thought of another man in her life was something she hadn't really allowed. It was work enough to make a living for her and her son. But whether she wanted to think about it or not she was still married, and some deep-seated part of her still held onto the idea that Jonah might return one day to make things right. Though that seemed less likely with each passing day.

She shook her head. She had no business at all thinking about Mr. Holt, or how the weight of his body on hers had made her feel, and how the tender touch of his lips had left her speechless. And while it had been something of an accident that had embarrassed her, she'd simply brushed her skirts and watched as he'd punched the other man, lifted the reins to the horses he had with him and walked right back out of town as if the fight had been nothing at all. So how was it her lips still tingled and the image of his soft brown eyes found her each night?

Lands, she needed to focus on her work, after all if it came down to it, she was still a married woman.

Chapter Two

Caleb scanned across town as he arrived in Wylder, the morning sun promising it to be a hot one. He urged Jericho through town toward the saloon, figuring he'd find his uncle Russ inside. The old cowboy was fond of his whiskey and set in his ways, but sometimes needed a good swift kick to the pants to remind him to lay off the rotgut.

He dismounted and tied his horse, glancing back at Cane Anson, one of the hands who held the reins of two Morgans they had brought to town to sell. A man from Denver had already wired the cash for the pair and said he'd be on the weekly stage by noon to ride them back home, the train fair too steep for the return trip.

"Wait here, huh?" Caleb spoke to the hand who gave a nod, Cane always quiet but loyal, a middle-aged man who had worked the ranch since way before Caleb was born.

Caleb stepped through the swinging doors of the saloon and was met by saloon owner, Sonny Cash, who arched a brow toward the corner and continued sweeping the hardwoods at the Five Star Saloon.

Caleb let out a heavy breath. His uncle sat in the corner at one of the tables, his head down, sleeping off the night before. Well, at least he wasn't sleeping it off in the local brothel. The madam, Miss Adelaide, didn't allow his uncle to stay the night when the place was

15

busy. She prided herself on the care of the girls in the business and couldn't focus when Russ hung around too long.

He made his way over and laid a hand on Russ's shoulder, shaking him gently. "Hey." Some part of him began to crush inside at how this seemed to play out more and more often. "Come on Uncle Russ, time to get ya' home."

The old man moaned, the smell of stale whiskey lingering as he began to move.

"Come on." Caleb grabbed his elbow and helped him stand, though Russ bobbled and shook until he was steady on his feet with a single eye open.

"Ah, a man can drink when he wants to." His uncle grumbled. "Can't he? Sonny, one for the road."

Sonny shook his head and continued sweeping. "You're on borrowed time as it is, Holt. Gonna have to start charging ya' rent."

"Chargin' me nothing except what I'm buying." Russ mumbled with a chuckle, both eyes open now, though he grabbed his low back.

Caleb dug in his trouser pocket and laid several coins on the table. With a nod to the barkeep, he led Russ outside by the arm, not giving him much choice about that morning drink. "Seems you've spent enough time with Miss Adelaide of late, they need to rent you a room at her place if I know anything about it."

"Don't know what all the fuss is about," Russ defended, but walked toward his horse where Cane waited with the Morgans. "Miss Addie's a friend's all. You ever spent time talking to a woman, just talking? It's a real good thing. 'Bout time you look at doing that. Women are smarter than us men, ya' know, learn a little something every time. You should try it."

"Russ, you gotta back off on the whiskey and visits to Miss Addie. This is the third time this month we're bailing you out of the saloon on a drunk," Caleb scolded. "Ain't no good for ya' and you know it. Doc Sullivan keeps warning you that you're on borrowed time."

"Coyote turns a belly up himself as I recollect," Russ defended, struggling to mount up as Caleb gave him a boost. "He's mighty fond of visits to the social club, too."

"Yea, well, Doc ain't passed out on a table this morning," Caleb retorted.

Russ groaned, settling in the saddle, his eyes half open in the bright sunlight of morning.

"Ah, get him back and let him sleep it off." Caleb nodded to Cane who took the reins to Russ's horse, though his uncle snatched them back and urged his mount ahead.

Caleb grabbed the two Morgans and turned back toward town. He'd planned the trip to town for the sale, but he hadn't wanted to find Russ passed out in the saloon once more. Cane would get his uncle home and never say a word, loyalty outweighing the trouble his uncle could cause. Uncle Russ was his father's older brother by only a couple of years. The two had purchased the land and started the horse farm back before the war, before Caleb had been born, Holt Ranch becoming a name known all over the west.

Caleb clucked his tongue, urging Jericho to follow as he made his way toward the railroad, where the stage would come in around noon.

"Caleb, need a chat with ya'." Sheriff Earl Hanson

hobbled toward him on the street, the man's ailing knees slowing him down.

Caleb stopped, and behind him Jericho and the Morgans did the same. "Sheriff."

"You, uhm, got Russ headed on home I see." The lawman glanced down the road and back.

Caleb nodded, holding the man's gaze. "He'll sleep it off, took care of his tab."

"Aw, I'm not too worried about your uncle much, but Tucker Johnson filed against you next morning after you took the horse back." The sheriff waited, kicking at the dirt.

That was of little surprise. "Let me guess. Horse thief?"

The sheriff's brows lifted in acknowledgment, along with the curl of his lips.

"You know better than that. He got his money back, minus the ointment I needed to treat the mare's hide." Caleb eyed the lawman he'd known all his life.

"Yep, I suppose I do. But Caleb, you can't take a horse back like that if a man pays you," the man kept his voice low.

Caleb held his gaze for a long moment. "I knew better than to sell the bay to him, could kick my own ass for that. He was warned."

"Johnson's holding a bit of a grudge, wants the horse back. Might be I can ease it over, get him to drop the charges, but he filed about his injuries as well since you knocked him clean out."

He started forward, but the sheriff stopped him, a palm to his chest. "He tossed the first punch, and I warned him about that, too. He ain't getting the horse back." Caleb glanced down at the man's hand on his chest. "Best you can do is your job and run him out of town."

"Look, I'm not gonna let the charges go through, but I don't need another brawl and Johnson knocked out again. He's pressing charges of assault and wants his medical bills to the doc paid." The sheriff waited on his nod.

"What's the doc's charges?" Caleb glanced at his scabbed knuckles. He supposed he had packed quite a punch, but the man had been warned more than once.

"'Bout four dollars. Doc had to stitch his brow and chin." The lawman grinned. "I know you like to do things on your own, take care of business, but you gotta stop taking back horses from men who do them wrong. Not much you can do once they own it and I'm gonna retire at some point. The next sheriff that comes through here won't see it the same. Might just call you a horse thief and…hang you."

"Next man comes along who harms a horse will get the same," Caleb defended. "And you'll have to arrest me where you see fit."

Hanson shook his head. "You're your father's son."

Caleb gave a nod as he rolled off four dollars from the paper money he pulled from his trousers.

"I'll pay the doc and run Johnson out of town soon enough." He angled a glance at Caleb. "Stage is running early. Got a wire, be here any minute with your buyer from Denver."

Caleb's gaze drifted as a woman crossed the street behind the lawman, who glanced the same direction. "Same lady you knocked down the other day."

Caleb lost sight of her, turning back to the

conversation. "That was by accident. You know her?"

Earl Hanson nodded. "Been in town a while now, got a small boy she carries around. Works in the dress shop, keeps to herself mostly."

"She married?" Caleb realized his slip when the older man chuckled.

The lawman glanced behind him again. "Haven't seen any man around, word has it she's on her own. Any reason you'd ask?"

Caleb narrowed his gaze on the man but said nothing.

"How about make sure this Denver sale gets to keep what he's paid for." Hanson turned to go, bending to rub one of his knees.

"Got it." Caleb continued on, the three horses following him past the depot. He grabbed a glance down Sidewinder Lane to the dress shop where the woman must have gone inside.

Hell, he had no time for a woman with all he had going on anyway, though thoughts of settling down with the right woman were something he'd always thought might have happened before now. It wasn't like there were many women in Wylder who weren't squaw, whore, or married. But he'd not soon forgotten the feel of the seamstress beneath him, nor had he forgotten the sweet taste of her plump lips. Hell, he was walking right in to quicksand with his thoughts.

****

The early rush of town, even on a Sunday always surprised Laurel. She stepped from the last stair onto the streets of Wylder heading toward the livery, Jesse on her hip and a picnic lunch in her bag, along with a few sugar cubes for Pink who would expect them.

It was early, but she gave a bit of a nod to two women who passed her, probably heading to church. She spotted Pink already saddled and waiting outside the corral as she arrived at the livery, most likely Mr. Daniel's doing. She'd paid her fees for the month and he said he would have the horse waiting.

"Piiinnnnnnk." Jesse gave a shrill cry reaching for the horse.

"Here you go." Laurel sat him on the animal and gave Pink a lump of sugar which the horse crunched loudly, nosing for more.

"Good mornin', Ms. Adams." Mr. Daniels approached, hat in hand.

"Thank you for saddling her up." She mounted up behind Jesse with ease.

"Might'n be you need to see about purchasing a small buggy soon for these rides you take on Sundays, ma'am." He gave her a hard look. "Got a small one I can sell ya' for around sixteen dollars, though it needs a bit of work. "I can do that for ya' as well."

She admired the horse and turned back to him. "Pink has never pulled a buggy, and besides, we enjoy the ride. I am very well acquainted with horses and riding, sir." It was true. Pink had been her horse before she had married. All those lonely days in the mining camp that still haunted her at times, it had been Pink that had held a brightness for her each day, at least until Jesse had come along.

The man gave the horse a pat. "Well, I reckon I don't have to warn you about riding out of town alone once more."

"We'll be more than fine, besides it's not so far where we're going." With that she clucked her tongue and gave Mr. Daniels a nod and headed Pink out of town on Old Cheyenne Road.

Jesse held the reins for a time with her assistance. She'd been teaching him how to guide the horse, though he was a bit young still at two and a half.

"Horsey. Fast. Mama." Jesse sat where she placed him before her, excited to be on the horse once more, his small legs kicking to urge Pink.

"Let's go, Pink." She giggled and the horse drew into a canter and then a slow gallop.

Jesse laughed, hanging on until she slowed the horse where the road turned to more of a trail and the edge of a tree line grew.

"Want to play in the water today?" She made small talk with her son, missing him being tiny but at the same time interested in him learning to do new things. He was smart and knew a lot more than he could say, but he already loved books and using chalk on the small slate she'd purchased at the mercantile.

She eased Pink to a slow canter when the meadow came into view. It wasn't a long ride, just about half an hour to the creek she'd discovered the summer before.

"Hang on, baby." She put his hand on the saddle horn and he held tight with another giggle as she dismounted and led the horse farther through the high grass, inhaling deeply. She smiled, happy for the sun riding her skin, the warmth welcome and somehow freeing.

The horse eased her nose to Laurel's pocket nudging her.

"Silly girl, you've already had your treat." Laurel dug two sugar cubes out and held them up to Pink who took them and chewed, following her.

"Nope, more next time, Pink." She tugged the horse ahead toward the stream and stopped her, lifting Jesse to the ground, where he trotted toward the soft flowing water.

She'd found this spot and now she liked to think it was her own little hiding place, a small escape from the reality of her situation, though she did pride herself on having survived and making a living for herself and her son. And days like today were her reward.

She let go of Pink, who followed her anyway and bent her large head to drink from the stream.

Jesse tugged on her pants, glancing up. "Shoes off, Mama?"

"All right, you can take your shoes off." She bent and he sat for her to untie his brown boots, which were getting near to being too small. She removed his stockings, tickling his toes until he snickered. She then untied her own riding boots and took them off along with her stockings, and took a moment to roll up both their britches. The stream wasn't deep at all, just a small trickle about two feet wide but it was full of beautiful soft round pebbles.

Jesse gave a shrill scream as he stomped and splashed, playing at the edge of the water, his light brown hair blowing in the summer wind.

She stepped into the cool creek and shuddered a gasp. It took a moment to get used to it, but after a minute it felt nice and would cool them when the afternoon heat came on stronger. She turned back to the horse and watched Jesse out the corner of her eye, and began removing the horse's saddle, then sat it by the large oak near the stream.

Pink nudged her. "I have no more sugar for you,

silly horse. Come on, girl."

She tugged the horse by the reins to hobble her nearby to graze and returned to the saddle to grab her bag. Keeping an eye on Jesse as he picked up rocks to toss into the water, she found the blanket she'd brought along and spread it beside the saddle. She hung her bag on a tree limb where Jesse couldn't reach it, being she carried the pistol. They would have their picnic a bit later but for now she turned to step back into the stream near her son.

"Mama." Jesse handed her a rock and she made great effort at tossing it into the water and laughing as it splashed.

He handed her another. "Mama's rock."

"Oh, thank you, kind sir." She tossed the next rock as he threw his own and gave a belting belly laugh.

She reached for a small stone that caught the sun and sparkled.

"Mama." Suddenly, Jesse grabbed to her leg, startled.

Laurel turned, a rider coming up on them at a slow gallop. She stepped toward her bag as he stopped the horse and dismounted. She made a lunge, grabbing the wrapped pistol, taking aim. "That's far enough."

Good Lord, this was the first time anyone had ever come up on her and Jesse at the river and she'd never had the weapon out of her bag. She did her best to steady her hand, aiming the gun, her heart in her throat. But as the rider got closer, it was none other than Caleb Holt on the horse coming their way.

He held his hands up. "Didn't mean to startle you. You…uh…won't need your gun, ma'am, but if you're planning to use it, you'll need to cock it. I'm Caleb

Holt."

"That would be the same Mr. Holt who knocked me to the ground recently." She lowered the pistol and reached the cloth to wrap it once more. Given his reputation she was sure she wouldn't need it.

He gave a slight nod.

She studied him for a long moment. "My name is Laurel Adams and this is Jesse, my son."

"I didn't mean that to happen and I did apologize." He held her gaze with those soft brown eyes that somehow reminded her of Jesse's.

She narrowed her brows with the shake of her head as she spoke. "No, as I recall you only apologized for taking a kiss without my permission." Was she being too forward in almost teasing about it?

He stepped closer, a grin spreading across his unshaven face. "Guilty, but I think I'll call us about even."

Jesse must have decided things were fine and went back to tossing stones into the creek.

"Even?" Laurel placed the weapon back into her bag, cinching it tight.

"Yep, seeing you're trespassing on my property." He glanced around them and back to her, holding up an arm in showing. "Holt Ranch, as far as you can see."

Laurel's mouth fell open. She hadn't known the creek was owned by anyone. "I'm sorry, I didn't know we were, this was, your...we'll just be on our way then."

"Whoa, hold up, it's fine, let your boy keep playing." He took his hat off. "It's probably nice to step away from town for a bit, especially for a little one. I've seen you both here before. But I recognized you from town and I did want to make sure you were all right."

"I was unharmed but we don't wish to be any trouble," she answered, wondering how often he had been watching them.

The curl to his lips was genuine. "No trouble and no harm done then, let him play anytime you come here."

"Thank you. I'm afraid with my work there isn't much time or place for him to play nor for me to give my horse a good run." She nodded, turning back to him, but keeping an eye on Jesse as well. "Your ranch is the one selling thoroughbreds?"

He fumbled with the hat in his hands. "I have a variety of breeds. Good lines but most out here aren't looking for more than a good work horse. Got a few draft animals too, for pulling loads. That's quite a beauty you have there in the Appaloosa."

And in spite of herself she allowed a smile. "I call her Pink. She's very gentle but has a feisty spirit." She walked with him toward the horse and gave her a rub.

He nodded as if for her permission and let a hand run across the horse's withers. "Where'd you get her?"

Laurel chose her words carefully. He was a handsome man and she found her lips recalling the sensation of his abrupt kiss. He wore a gun and he had shoulder length brown hair and deep brown eyes to match, a sprinkle of stubble across his chin. "My family is from Tennessee. My father raised horses and he gave her to me…before I came west."

He let his gaze cover the horse. "Well she's gonna need to be shod coming up."

"Yes, Mr. Daniels at the livery has let me know the same, only I've to wait a bit for saving the money," she answered. "I work in Lowery's Dress Shoppe and the Widow Lowery only pays once per month."

In the distance, another cowboy called from above the ridge, an echo following. "Holt."

He tossed up an arm and moved back to his quarter horse and mounted up. "Bring her out here next Sunday and I'll shoe her for ya'. No charge. Least I can do."

Laurel held his gaze. He'd already kissed her and now caught her trespassing, and what if he shod Pink for free? What would he expect in return? "Thank you, but I'm afraid I cannot accept your hospitality. I will soon have enough for her to be shod."

He gave a nod, his brown eyes kind if nothing more. "You change your mind, just let me know. My men ride through here now and again, no one's gonna bother you or your boy when you come here."

"Thank you." Laurel spoke, but she couldn't fully let down her trust. She'd learned quick about the men found in Wylder. They all had a story and they were all the same in their wants when it came down to it. So why did she watch until Caleb Holt had ridden out of sight?

Laurel turned back to the old tree, making sure the bag remained out of Jesse's reach before returning to the stream to play with him.

"Mama. Eat now." Jesse trotted toward her.

"Are you hungry? Go sit on the blanket." She pulled the lunch sack from her bag and unwrapped the sandwiches she'd made earlier that morning. She sat and put a small plate before Jesse who folded his hands.

"Bless us dear lord for this bounty. Amen." She said a quick prayer, her pulse still racing from the visit with Mr. Holt.

"Amen." Her son echoed, making her smile though he quickly opened the bread and took the meat in one hand and the cheese in the other, shoving both hands toward his mouth.

"Careful. Eat a little at a time." She watched as he chewed, though he did a fine job of the mouthful he had taken. She began eating but reached for the small rocks beside him, laying three in a row. "Count with me. One, two, three."

She pointed to each rock and he copied her.

"One, two, tree." He didn't quite get three right, but she praised him anyway.

"Good boy. Again."

He stuffed his mouth, chewing and speaking, his words muffled as he pointed to each rock once more.

"Good boy. You're so very smart." She tousled his hair and watched as Pink moved to graze, though her mind drifted back to Mr. Holt. He'd been kind in allowing continued visits here, but her trust of men, any man, wasn't to come easy ever again. She glanced at Jesse, who was done and got up to walk into the high grass. It seemed Mr. Holt had seen her before now and she wasn't sure how she felt about that. How long had he been watching her and her son at the creek? But a better question was why her lips continued to tingle as if in anticipation of the kiss that hadn't taken her this time.

Chapter Three

After a long day riding to Cheyenne and back, where he'd picked up a couple of mustang mares, Caleb arrived back at the ranch. He hadn't been sure he'd make the purchase, but as he stopped Jericho outside the corral, he eyed the two mares, satisfied he'd gotten a good price for both. These two would help breed new lines for the ranch.

"Guessin' you paid a golden nickel for those two." Uncle Russ exited the barn, dusting the hay from his trousers, a big grin across his face and more than a day's whiskers along his cheeks.

"About what you thought." Caleb dismounted, lifted his hat and wiped his brow of the heat and dirt with his sleeve. "A good pair. Looks like you finally slept it off. You hurt?"

Russ ambled closer, holding his low back and running a hand down one of the mares. "No, I ain't hurt, just bent."

Caleb chuckled, as any time his uncle spent time at the Social Club with Miss Addie, he nearly threw his back out. "Long night at the Social Club then?"

Russ gave him a scolding gaze. "Shut the hell up."

Caleb nodded. "You're avoiding the question."

His uncle turned away, cursing under his breath. "No sense haggling over the same old things."

He held the man's gaze with a hard look. "Well,

Cane brought you back for haggling a little too long in town again. Passed out cold this time. Doc's already warned it's gonna kill ya."

Russ inhaled a deep breath and let it out with a chuckle. "Haggling a little more than alcohol this time is what's done me in. I'm good."

Caleb held his Uncle's gaze and coiled up the rope he'd been gathering. "It takes us both to run this ranch, and we lose a day from you every time you hang in the saloon, not to mention the evenings spent in the Social Club."

"I'm here now. But seems I'm not the only one doing a little bit of riding fences." His uncle narrowed a hard look at him. "Who is she?"

Caleb turned to the mares, opening the corral and urging them inside, releasing their leads one at a time. Both were a bit nervous and ran to the far side of the corral.

"Now who's avoiding the question? Cane said you told them a woman would be picnicking occasional Sundays down by the creek and to leave her be." Russ closed the gate and turned to face him with a lift of his gray brows.

Hell, it wasn't some big thing to worry over. "She's just a woman. She's been coming to the creek to let her son play by the water, get him out of town. Not much more than that."

Russ gave him a slap on the back and a hint of a knowing more than he should. "Uh hum."

Caleb shook his head and grabbed Jericho's reins. "Look, just don't run her off if you see her."

"Nope, sure won't do that, but you came on back from Cheyenne quick. Planning on a nice Sunday ride?" Russ snickered and turned back toward the barn "That's right. I know more than you think I do. She's been here a good bit and you been watching, minding the fences that way."

This time Caleb cursed under his breath. He was tired from the trip. It was hot as hell today and if it came to it, he was downright starving. But he'd spent over a week with nothing but Laurel Adams on his mind. He had seen her several times with her son at the creek over the months but until last Sunday, he'd never stopped to see who she was. A woman with a small child was of little harm. He hadn't known she was the woman he'd knocked down in town and then kissed. But it was true that not much happened on Holt land that Russ didn't know about.

He turned back to his work, though Laurel's face rode his mind. She was damn as beautiful a woman as he'd ever seen and even though her hair had been pulled up on her head every time he'd seen her, it had blown a bit into a disarray of curls in the light summer breeze. He imagined it a lot longer than it seemed, but her eyes were as captivating as he'd ever known. Such a deep green they matched the darkest of leaves in the summer trees and the pines of winter.

But there was more to her, something more she wasn't telling. When he'd first fallen across her in town, she'd had on a fancier dress than most women and it seemed the riding pants and boots she wore weren't items that came cheap. She wasn't like the women in and around Cheyenne, almost as if she didn't belong, and he'd detected a bit of an English accent in speaking with her, intriguing him all the more. And while it seemed he was losing his mind in falling for

Laurel Adams, there was a horse that needed to be shod and he was just the man that was gonna do it—if she'd let him.

****

The afternoon haze of heat took its toll as Caleb rode in from the southern pastures, turned Jericho toward the river, wondering if Laurel Adams would be there. Laurel. It was an unusual name but seem to fit her, a bit of hidden feistiness in a woman who was rather quiet. Of course she had pulled a pistol on him, but it didn't seem she knew much about using it.

He hadn't promised to be at the river and he'd spent a damn long week wondering if it had been on her mind as well. He slowed Jericho. Spending the day out checking on each of the horses could be long, the forty animals he had in the western pastures often spread out, but he'd found the two mustang mares, adjusting fine to being with the others.

With several expectant mares, he had Cane and Ed out checking the other pastures and herding the expectant mothers in closer at night. Ed Cartwright, like Cane, had been with Holt Ranch since the beginning. Both hands and his uncle lived in the bunkhouse just off the main barn in a thicket of trees.

He eyed the structure, a couple of miles out, from the height of the ridge he was crossing. It seemed Russ was coming home more and more often on a drunk. He shook his head. Wasn't gonna be long until his uncle came home dead at the rate he was going.

He eased Jericho to the main trail toward the small stream, keeping to the shady trees that led the way. He'd lost his father several years back from his years of smoking. If things didn't change, he'd lose his uncle to alcohol. Russ was all Caleb had left, but there were reasons the man drank, though neither his father nor his uncle had ever spoken of it. He'd never understood it until one day Cane had explained it to him when they were putting his drunk Uncle Russ to bed.

His father and uncle had fallen in love with the same woman—Caleb's mother. And Uncle Russ had left the territory. It wasn't until Sarah Holt died that Russ had returned to the ranch that was half his. His father had never said a word but had worked alongside his brother as if nothing at all had changed.

He glanced back at the ranch house as it faded from view. He lived alone in that big damn house and sometimes he swore he could hear the walls talking, it was so quiet. But Russ had never made the move inside, even after his father had passed. He reckoned that was due to the memory and pictures of his mother.

Caleb stopped Jericho. Ahead at the small stream, Laurel sat on a blanket, her son sleeping nearby. He dismounted, watching her for a moment. She leaned against the old tree that shaded the ground, reading a book. His breath caught as she tugged a strand of loose hair behind her ear and turned the page. He wasn't sure he should interrupt her, but at least she had returned and he'd brought what he needed to shoe her horse, hobbled in the same shady area.

He moved closer on foot, tugging Jericho by the reins. As he approached, she turned and after a moment, a smile crossed her lips. Well, that was a surprise, as if she might have been waiting on him. He tied off the horse in the nearby shaded shrubs and lifted the wooden box from the back of the saddle, tossing the strap over his shoulder.

She stood as he got closer. She was wearing pants and riding boots, the kind that were expensive, making him wonder about her means or her past. She knew horses, something surprising for a woman, and with the way she dressed, she'd had money at one time.

"I wondered if you might ride by." She spoke first in a slight whisper, glancing at her sleeping son and back to him.

He waited until he was close to her and whispered, "Got a horse to shoe."

She glanced at Pink, shaking her head. "I'll have the money soon enough. I wasn't expecting…"

"Nonsense. Now you can use the money for something more you need." He nodded as he turned toward the animal.

"All right then, but only if you'll share our lunch. I made extra as we usually make a day of it." She followed him toward the horse. "I've been told someone paid my bill ahead at the livery. I was wondering if you might know something of that as well."

Caleb glanced at her again. "Just trying to apologize for knocking you down and for the trouble of embarrassing you. Chet Daniels owed me a bit to my account. I'd be obliged for the meal though." He lifted the horse's front hoof between his knees and pulled the necessary tools from the bucket.

He'd make short work of shoeing one horse; as he was used to shoeing several in a row at the ranch. "She's right tame, not even resisting."

"Pink has always been gentle, though she loves to run. It's hard for me to take her on a real run with Jesse, though." She ran her hand along the horse, and a bit of his focus gave. "I used to watch my father do what you're doing."

"Oh, yeah?" He glanced up and back to his work. "Whereabouts?"

"I'm from Tennessee, middle of the state. We had a few horses, nothing like your ranch, I'm afraid." She spoke in a normal voice now that she'd stepped away from her sleeping son, and he was sure he could hear the English accent.

"We got a couple of hundred in the herds now, I'm working on growing that." He measured the shoe he'd use for the animal and trimmed a bit more. "Seems we've a bit in common. My father and uncle came from Chattanooga long before the war, started Holt Ranch."

"It's a small world then," she added. "Though my mother was from England."

He chuckled. "I was thinking you had a British accent. I was born here, don't know much other than the territory. How'd you end up out here?"

She took a deep breath and spoke more slowly as if she were choosing careful words. "I married Jesse's father and we were to find our way to a homestead, though all we found was the mining camp north of here. He'd aspirations of a gold strike and I found myself alone most of the time. Of course, there was never to be a homestead." She rounded Pink as he worked the next hoof.

"I woke one morning and he was simply gone. I'm sure you heard the gossip in town." She shook her head, a bit of a blush turning her cheeks.

Caleb bent to the horse. So she'd had a husband but not anymore, not a surprise since she had a child. "Not much for town gossip, though I'm sure there's plenty on me as well."

She stood there, most likely waiting on an explanation, the sun catching her hair and her skin as smooth as satin.

He swallowed hard and turned back to the horse and continued. "I hold men to their word and the care of my horses when they purchase. Sometimes that don't go as planned." He leaned down to move the bucket closer. "My family has been selling horses here long enough for the Holt name to stand for something. And you ended up in Wylder when he left."

She took a deep breath, glancing away. "I knew he wasn't going to return. He took the little money we had, though he left me with Jesse, Pink, and my mother's sewing machine. Wylder was closer than elsewhere. I found work here and I suppose the rest is history." She folded her arms and watched as he worked. Damn, keeping his eyes from her was tough. He could watch her all day if there were a day made for it.

"Not much in a man who would do something like that," Caleb said as he placed the second shoe to the horse, uncertain he should toss such easy words.

"I suppose I knew all along it would happen that way." She didn't look at him but glanced back at Jesse who was beginning to stir from his slumber.

"Why didn't ya go back home to Tennessee?" he asked, curious more than anything else.

She moved a bit closer. "I've no family left there to speak of and I suppose at first I thought Jonah might return, though that hasn't happened."

He nodded and nailed the shoe in place. The note of sadness in her voice tore at him. "Well, all I got here's my uncle Russ, drinks too much but he most often means well. A good man."

She glanced at Jesse who turned to his back, but still slept. "He runs the ranch with you?"

"Raised me along with my father after my mother died. Lost my father several years back. Russ and me, we make a good team." Why was talking with her easier than he'd expected? He finished up with the animal and gathered his tools, tossing them into the bucket again. The work had come fast with the bit of nerves he carried in making small talk with her. He stood again, holding her gaze. She was a real beauty, her hair pulled up, her skin tanned from the outdoors, and those deep green eyes.

"Well, it's very beautiful here, but not so much in town," she added. "I appreciate that we can spend time here each week."

He gave the horse a pat.

Just then Laurel startled, stepping away. "Jesse!"

Caleb turned. The boy laughed, clapping his hands at having climbed boulders at the creek's edge along the small cliffs. Caleb ran toward the rocks, Laurel just behind him, and scaled up the boulders in what seemed like seconds. "Gotcha." He grabbed the boy into his arms

Jesse giggled, reaching for his mother as Caleb climbed back to the ground.

"Oh, thank God. Jesse, you will fall off the rocks. You may not climb there again," she scolded before hugging the boy to her body.

"No, no rocks," Jesse mimicked, looking back at him.

"You'll get hurt." She put him back to his feet and he scampered off to see what was in Caleb's bucket of tools.

"Jesse, please…" Laurel tried to tug him away. "The tools will harm you as well."

"It's fine, Ms. Adams, nothing much there gonna hurt him." Caleb lifted the clippers and shaver out of the way and put them in his saddle bags. "He can play there."

Laurel nodded, and he caught himself watching her admire her son. "I had thought he was a handful when he was small, but now he's on the run most all the time. I have to hang onto him or carry him in town. I'm afraid he'll run into the streets."

"Reckon town isn't much place for a boy his size," he added.

"Well, do come, I'm sure you're hungry as you've said. Jesse. Let's go eat." She made herself busy as Caleb removed his hat and sat beside the blanket on the ground. In the shade of the overgrowth of trees, he simply watched her until she spoke to her son, who bounced close by and sat near her.

"Jesse, you should say thank you to Mr. Holt for getting you down from the rocks." She handed her son a small plate with bread and meat.

"Sa-e." The little boy tried. He was a handsome little boy with light brown hair and brown eyes, dressed in trousers, shirt, and boots.

"You are welcome, sir." Caleb held out a hand to the toddler.

Jesse looked at his hand and then to his mother. "Mama?"

"It's all right, you're getting to be a big boy, shake Mr. Holt's hand." She nodded toward Caleb.

The little boy leaned closer and as quick as a flash

touched Caleb's hand. He drew back with a smile and did so again, but this time Caleb held the boy's tiny hand longer. "Boy, that's a strong grip you got there."

Jesse laughed.

"How old is he?" He asked.

"Jesse, how old are you?" She placed the question to her son.

He chuckled. "Tree." He then bowed his head and clasped his fingers. "Amen."

She smiled, this time her teeth shining white as she bowed her head and then glanced up. "Amen. He's almost three."

"He's a right handsome boy, smart too." Caleb took the plate from her. "Hadn't expected real plates and a napkin," which he laid across his knee. Manners, something he'd rarely thought about for a long time.

"Well, if I've learned anything out here, it's to use the fine china." She lifted her brows as she shook her head. "At least what's left of it."

"Accident?" He asked as he began on his meal, thinking the china wasn't a cheap set.

"Well, a wagon down a steep incline with a crate of dishes doesn't always fare too well. I managed to save a few pieces of each item, plates, saucers, and cups."

"It's not an easy trail around here." He chewed and swallowed.

"None of this has been easy, but Jesse and I are doing well enough, I suppose." She handed her son a small apple. "See if Mr. Holt would like an apple, Jesse."

The boy eyed him again and leaned closer, handing the apple to him and then holding out his hand for another which she gave to him.

"Horsie." It was Jesse who pointed to the far edges of the ridge.

Caleb jumped up and squinted. There was a mustang herd in the distance. "Son of a…" He stopped himself short, forgetting he was in the presence of a lady.

"Are they yours?" she asked as she stood alongside him.

"It's a wild herd." He moved away from them both, spotting The Black, the stallion he'd had his eye on for a couple of years now. The midnight black mustang also carried a contrasting white mane and tail making him easy to spot. But the creature was somehow magical, elusive, and not a man who'd ever tried had gotten him.

The herd hadn't been in this area in over a year. Maybe this time, he'd be on The Black and bring the stallion to Holt's Ranch to get some of that mustang fire into the herds he owned. But as quickly as they had moved in, they were lost over the rise. He turned back toward the quilt. "Sorry, just been following that herd for a bit, not a man in the territory that hasn't been looking for The Black."

"The stallion?" She questioned as she sat once more.

He nodded, focusing as best he could for the moment, his pulse racing. This woman knew horses well, as he'd already discovered. "Been waiting on him to bring the herd back this way for over a year now."

Jesse pointed again. "Horsie gone."

"The horses will be back, Jesse, eat your meat and we can play." Laurel handed his plate to him once more though the little boy focused on him. "Black?"

Caleb held the little boy's gaze. "Yep, the black horse is the fastest horse in the West by my figuring. You spotted him first, Jesse."

"Black horsie fast." The little boy grinned in satisfaction.

"He loves horses, always has, I suppose because we have Pink." Laurel bit into one of the apples, chewing slowly. Not staring at her was rather difficult when it came down to it. And while he'd never thought much of his future with a wife, this woman was enough to make him think hard on the idea.

"You seem to really know horses, given…" He stopped, not wanting her to find offense.

"Given I'm a woman?" She grinned with a lift of her brows.

"Well, most women here know a good work horse, but you seem to know a great deal more and given your boots there, you at one time were around the animals a lot, if I am not assuming too much." He was sure he'd figured a thing or two if he could get her talking as now.

She studied him for a long moment. "I told you my father had horses but if you are insinuating I come from money, then you'd be right. At least at one time I did."

Caleb didn't comment, but he wasn't surprised.

"Actually, my father was wealthy, raised horses that raced, prided himself on the lines he built and made his fortune." She stared off in the distance as she continued. "But somehow money isn't everything. When my mother fell ill, there was nothing that could be done and so he stuck his head in a bottle and never came up for air. He lost most of what he'd gained through his entire life. I managed to help him sell what

41

he did have, to keep the house, but I'd met Jonah by then and I don't know, maybe it was my way out. Father died the following year and that would be all there is to tell. There was no money left, making me wonder why it should be so important to work so hard in life to then allow it to all fall away to nothing."

Caleb nodded, but it seemed maybe he'd touched a tender subject. "I should apologize for pushing, but I did notice your boots. They don't make boots like that out here."

She touched the leather of the upper suedes. "They were purchased in England by my mother and they have weathered well, but I make most of my clothing, and you owe me no apology for being curious. But tell me of you?"

He narrowed his gaze and began, not that much about his life was interesting. "Raised out here like I said, mostly worked horses but my father insisted on a good education, did some time at school in Denver for post studies. Hated it but finished and came back home to manage things here. Pa got sick and so me and Russ have kept it all going and it's continued to be successful."

She wiped Jesse's mouth with one of the napkins. "But you never married, nor Russ?"

He shook his head, a forward question to ask. "Guess I've stayed too busy or never found the right woman. Russ is complicated. He and my father fell in love with the same woman, my mother, and so Russ left for years. Seems he had a family, a wife and daughter that died in a fire while he was out hunting. I never knew them. He's never told me about it, probably isn't even aware that I know, but I think maybe that's why he's heavy on the rotgut as well. He's a good man, though, but I'm worried it's gonna kill him. Doc's told him to back off the booze and the ladies, but he's as ornery as they come. He don't much like me keeping on him about it."

"It was the same with my father, but addiction like that is difficult to put behind." She shrugged. "I tried hiding the bottles, pouring them out, but there was always more."

He nodded. "Guess we both know what it's like then, why I rarely drink."

"Mama." Jesse handed her his plate and got up to walk back to the stream.

Caleb finished his sandwich, enjoying the quiet and being in her presence and the fact they were sharing a bit about each other. He hadn't expected that so soon.

He remembered the damn napkin and wiped his mouth when she pointed to her own cheek with a nod. "Sorry."

"No worries, but I do thank you again for Pink's care. The money saved will help since Jesse is in need of new boots." She laughed as her son ran in the high grass, calling to her.

"Mama, Mama." Jesse whirled. "Run."

"He wants to play," Caleb added, looking on as the little boy ran and laughed.

"Yes." She laid their plates aside. "Come, you can run with us…" She grasped his hand, tugging him to his feet, before he could comprehend her touching him with her delicate hand. Damn, he'd not held a woman's hand in years. She let go as she chased her son, and he followed, caught up in her and Jesse's laughter.

The boy roared and showed his hands like claws,

baring his teeth. "I bear." He ran at her and she pretended to scream and run as her son chased her. Caleb laughed at the display, aware Laurel had turned to watch him.

He did the same, growling and acting like a giant bear. "Nope, I am the biggest bear." He roared and trotted toward them both, making them scatter.

Jesse gave a shrill scream, but couldn't run due to his hard belly laughs, so Caleb roared again, scooped the boy up and ran after Laurel. He roared louder and Jesse laughed and kicked urging him on. As he caught up to Laurel, he put Jesse down. "Run little bear, get her."

Jesse took off, grabbing his mother by the leg until she spun and sat in the high grass, pulling him to her and tickling him.

He stopped before them and Jesse took off again. Laurel was up and running after him, though the boy turned back for a bite of his meal, and then ran to rub Pink. The horse remained unamused and continued chomping on the grass.

Caleb reached out and tagged a hand to Laurel's shoulder. He growled and she screamed and fell into the grass. He landed beside her and time stood still once more, reminding him of when he had fallen across her in town.

"We do keep finding ourselves like this," she whispered, making him wonder if the kiss he'd like again was welcome.

Her breath heaved along with his, and he leaned in and placed his lips to hers, fully expecting her to greet his cheek with her palm. He lifted away and stared at her lips, her cheeks, and then her deep green eyes.

He let his lips curl as well. "I thought maybe you'd slap me, think me too forward, but I won't apologize this time…"

She angled a glance at him. "Perhaps it's me who is being too forward for allowing it."

"No, I'd never think that, but I won't ever apologize, so if you don't want me to do that again, you'll have to tell me so." Damn, he wanted another taste, a moment to let his hands ride along her body.

Her lips parted slightly. "I'm still a married woman…"

He touched her lips with his thumb. "He's no husband if he ain't here to do what I just did." He took her lips then, parting them and tasting her fully, her deep moan his reward. It had been a long time since he'd kissed a woman and even longer since he'd…

He eased his hand down her body. Jesse plopped onto his back with a shrill bear roar.

Caleb rolled away, grabbing the boy and tossing him in the air and catching him as he sat.

Laurel sat up, tugging grass from her hair as Jesse bounced away again. "You're right about Jonah, my husband. I should have known early on, but I became with child, leaving me little in the way of choices. He does remain Jesse's father, here or not."

Caleb stood and took her hand and helped her up, her eyes full of questions he had no answers for. "How long's it been?"

She walked alongside him watching Jesse. "A year or so since he left us."

Hell, he damn well knew better than to toss words he didn't mean, but there was something about Laurel that made him see forever. "I'd like to see you again…spend time with you and Jesse, let us get to know each other."

Laurel bit her bottom lip. "But…"

He pulled her to him. "He left you, Laurel…and no one out here holds that legal." He had no right to belittle what she'd once had with her husband, but any man who would have left behind a woman like this couldn't have been in his right mind.

She leaned into him "I'd like that, Mr. Holt…time with you…"

Caleb's heart raced and he brought her face to his lips once more, kissing her with passion and holding her as tight as he dared. "Then we'll make that happen, but you have to call me by my name, Laurel."

She nodded, those green eyes focusing on him and rimmed with tears. "I'd like that very much, Caleb."

He hugged her, holding her for all the man he was worth and all the woman he knew her to be.

Chapter Four

Laurel strolled along the street holding Jesse's hand. The afternoon sun had begun to set, but she needed a few things at the Wylder Mercantile for making bread, and the new shoes she had ordered for Jesse had come in. In her other hand, she held Pink's reins and the horse lagged along behind them, content with a bit of a ride that hadn't taken them all the way to the stream, though she'd thought of it. She glanced into the sky where darker clouds were beginning to gather. She needed to get Pink back to the livery.

"Do you like your new shoes?" She glanced down at Jesse who could hardly walk for admiring the boots on his feet, brown and shiny.

He glanced up at her and pointed at the shoes. "Jesse's boots."

She nodded, "What color are they?"

He looked at them again and back to her. "Jesse's shoes brown."

"Yes, brown." She slowed their pace to glance into some of the windows of the town shops, always admiring this or that, but never purchasing much for herself. With Pink's fees paid and Jesse wearing his new shoes, she did have a bit extra, but other needs would surely arise. Thunder sounded in the distance and she increased her pace, thinking she'd best not dawdle.

"Howdy, ma'am." A man in a dark blue soldier's uniform stopped her, a cigar hanging from his mouth.

Laurel gave a simple nod, not speaking as she tugged Jesse and Pink to pass him.

"Seems a mite hot out and I's watching you and your son there walking through town, thought I could maybe talk to ya' a bit and get you a drink of cool water." He moved closer than was comfortable, the smoke from his cigar making her cough as Pink shied.

"Thank you, but we're quite fine." She gripped Jesse's hand and attempted to walk around him once more, but another man stepped out from the side alley she had been about to pass, blocking her way. Thunder echoed as the sky began to darken and the winds lifted.

Laurel hesitated, but the streets were quiet and there was no quick way to escape. Pink shied further and Laurel was losing her grip.

"Mighty pretty like you told me, Ike." The second soldier in uniform reached out to touch a strand of her hair. "Right soft, too."

"I beg your pardon, sir, you are out of line." Jesse began to cry, clinging to her leg.

"Now, ma'am, we're just wanting to talk a bit." He leaned closer and grabbed her arm shoving her toward the alley. Jesse fell to the ground near Pink.

Laurel struggled to free herself, fighting as the man pinned her to the wall his hands roaming her body. Nearby Jesse screamed, as both men held her still, one of the men trying to lift her skirt and the other covering her mouth with the taste of whiskey as he squeezed her breast. She swung her fists and hit one man's ear, the pain in her hand numbing.

The soldier cursed and raised his fist, smacking it

across her cheek and sending another blinding blow to her head. Her vision blurred and her thoughts spun as she fought to stay conscious.

Another smack came across her cheek and she tasted blood as her skirts were pushed higher.

No, they couldn't do this. She fought to push them away but another blow came and her head popped back. The hand squeezing her thighs rose higher. Her foot came up to meet the closest man's groin. He sent a fist into her side, knocking the air from her while the other man held her upright.

"No…Jesse." Her breath came in gasps and a fist was raised to her again. She took the blow, then bit down hard on the hand covering her mouth. Her knee came up to slam the second man's crotch. He doubled and fell away from her, falling to his knees and swearing.

Laurel swung again. She had to keep them from Jesse. The heel of her hand made contact with the other man's nose. He cursed as blood spurted forth. He slapped at her but she clawed at his face, screaming with all the force she could muster.

A gunshot filled the air and suddenly both men ran. Laurel fell back against the wall her chest heaving in exertion as she straightened her skirts. Jesse ran to her.

"Jesse…" She drew him up into her arms, comforting him as best she could.

"Ma'am are you all right?" A man eased closer to her as sprinkles of rain began and thunder cracked in the darkening sky. She turned to see a group of men from the saloon standing there. She supposed they had heard her screams, but she took Pink's reins from him.

"Thank you," she whispered, her own voice feeling

distant as she tried to make sense out of what had just happened.

"It's all right, Jesse, let's go back on Pink for a ride." She placed him in the saddle and then mounted up, unconcerned that her skirts rode high to her knees. Thunder echoing in the distance and a jagged streak of lightning lit the sky.

Her eyes filled with tears as she turned Pink. There was no time to think about what had just happened. The impending storm urged her to nudge Pink into a run out of town. She rode for the stream and toward Caleb's ranch. She didn't want to go home, not sure if it was safe there tonight. And she didn't want to be alone.

As she made the dirt road away from the buildings of Wylder, she pulled her shawl from her shoulders and wrapped it around Jesse.

Surely, she was insane. What if Caleb wasn't even there? Then again, what if he was? She was shaking, she supposed more frightened of what almost happened than what had, but for some reason all she could think of was falling into Caleb's arms.

Wrapped in the thick shawl, Jesse cried but held tight, the fabric protecting him from the hard pellets of hailing rain which took her breath and stung her face. The rain came harder and thunder rolled and cracked all around them. Tears began to blur her vision. Through it all, Pink held true, running as if she knew where to go.

Lightning streaked the prairie sky as she rode Pink to the high grass that led to the Holt ranch. Hail fell, the icy crystals pecking at her skin and now she knew her judgment to ride in this weather a mistake. She drew Jesse closer to her, though they were both drenched to the bone now. What had she been thinking, riding off in a storm? Hot tears scorched her cheeks in spite of the whipping winds and hail.

Thunder shook the earth beneath them. Jesse screamed, trying to climb into her arms. She could scarce hear his cries over the noise from the storm. She slowed Pink and pulled Jesse to her chest, gathering her bearings as she whispered soothing words.

She'd passed the stream; the ranch should be close. Shivering, she urged Pink ahead as more cold pellets of ice hailed down. Her hair hung in her face but she had no free hand to push it away as she struggled to see. Ahead the rain was a solid sheet of white before her. In the distance, the barn and main house were barely visible. A crack sounded overhead and a branch fell, hitting her head with enough force to near knock her from the horse. She bobbled and Pink slowed. Then she was falling, clinging tight to Jesse, her mind went blank and the cold, hard rain swallowed her to the ground.

****

Caleb rode Jericho into the big barn and dismounted, slinging water and hail from his hat.

Already inside, Russ moved closer to the barn doors to take a look at the summer storm. "This one's rough. Might be a wind tunnel."

Caleb brushed ice from the back of Jericho's saddle. "Did the boys bring it in? Ain't gonna get no work done in this kind of weather anyway."

Russ nodded, adjusting his hat and coiling a rope, hanging it on the hook by the barn door. "They came in about an hour ago. Got the fence mended on the south where the tree fell."

"Mares herded in?" Caleb asked. Most often in a heavy storm the pregnant mares were corralled or stalled in the barns if given time, but this storm had come out of nowhere.

"They'd time to get most in. A few stragglers." Russ shook his head. "Better shelter here till this passes...bad storm this one."

Caleb moved closer to Russ by the barn doors, the wind whipping around them. Movement in the distance caught his attention. "What the hell's that?"

Russ squinted "The tarnation?"

A small child, almost invisible in the solid sheet of hail and rain, ran toward the house...his brown coat all that made him visible as he barreled their way.

"Son of a bitch, it's Jesse." Caleb tore from the barn. Lightning zapped in the distance with hail pounding his flesh. He scooped the screaming boy against his shoulder, huddling as he glanced around for Laurel. Something wasn't right. She would never leave Jesse to his own, much less in a storm. The child was soaked through, crying hysterically, his little body shaking hard in the cold as Caleb turned and ran back into the barn.

Russ hurried toward him with a blanket. "Here."

Caleb wrapped Jesse in it and sat on one of the feed crates, cradling the boy in his lap. "Jesse. It's all right. Hey...come on. Let's warm you up." He rubbed his hair and arms to dry him.

He tried to ease the blanket around Jesse but the boy was clinging to him too tight. Caleb held him to his chest and gave him a minute. Jesse's cheeks were red where hail had pelted him. The toddler rubbed his head, still crying. "Jesse scared."

"It's all right. Where's Mama? Jesse." Caleb glanced at Russ who walked closer. He bent to a knee, rubbing Jesse's back.

Caleb lifted Jesse's head and the boy squalled again, trying to hide his face. "Jesse, where's Mama?"

Jesse sniffled and turned away from his chest and pointed back out to the storm still clinging to him. "Mama fall down."

Caleb rubbed the bruise that stood on the boys head, there being more than one. "Is Mama at the creek? Jesse, is Mama there by the stream where we play?"

The boy pointed again still rubbing his head. "Mama fall down by fence."

Caleb's heart sank. He shoved the hat beside him back on his head. "I gotta find her." He rose and held the child out to Russ. "Here, take him."

Jesse screamed and kicked though Russ kept him tight in the blanket, trying to console him as Caleb mounted up once more onto Jericho.

"Best you hurry. The hail's not letting up. I got him. Russ juggled Jesse, who still whimpered. "You go. I'll send the boys out to help."

He took off toward the stream, uncertain which fence Jesse meant. How on earth had the little boy made it on his own? Heart in his throat, he raced Jericho against the wind and the hail. He had to find her. Laurel. He turned toward the creek and slowed Jericho who was having a hard time of it.

Damnit. He scanned the horizon. How was he to find Laurel out here? Was she all right? What the hell had even happened to bring her out in this weather?

And then he saw Pink in the distance by the fence…holy hell. Jesse had known what he was saying. On the ground beside Pink lay Laurel, the loyal horse staying with her for protection, he supposed. He dismounted and ran to her.

She was on her side, her hair a muss over her face, and for a moment a streak of panic took him. What if she was…

"Laurel." He brushed her hair back, finding blood covering her brow and a huge whelping bruise there, but she moaned unmoving. She was alive. He glanced up as Cane and Ed rode closer, the rain pouring over them all.

"She hurt bad?" Cane asked as he dropped from his horse and ran over.

"Not sure. Hand her up to me and ride for the doc. Ed, take her horse, it could be injured. See if you can check her." Caleb mounted Jericho again and took Laurel across his lap as the men handed her up. He gave them a nod as Cane road toward town.

"Get her back. I got the horse." Ed shouted against the whipping of high winds. "It's a small twister…seen it from the bunkhouse."

Caleb adjusted Laurel across his knees and urged Jericho to a trot. She hadn't moved but she shivered even as he sheltered her with his coat. It had been a long time since he'd thought to utter a prayer, but he did so now.

****

Caleb stood outside his bedroom holding Jesse, who slept against his shoulder. The grandfather clock in the hallway sounded half past ten, and while it still trickled rain, the storm had subsided.

Doctor Sullivan was in with Laurel, and he had been holding Jesse who had promptly fallen asleep.

Russ had given the boy a warm bath to stave off

the cold and dressed him in one of Caleb's shirts, the boy unharmed.

Russ brought over a tin of black coffee. "Never seen a little one do what that one there did."

Caleb gestured to the table, and Russ sat the steaming brew aside. "It was right at a mile or more for him to make here. Not sure how he did it."

Russ nodded. "Saved her life most likely."

Caleb turned as Doctor Coyote Sullivan shut the door behind him. "She'll be all right. Got a pretty good concussion but nothing's broken. Must've been a hell of a branch that hit her but her vision's good. She wanted to see the boy. I assured her he was fine and gave her something to help her rest. Seems some soldiers got a little too forward with her. I got their descriptions and will let the sheriff know."

"Soldiers?" Caleb's pulse raced. They wouldn't need to worry about the sheriff once he found them.

Coyote raised a brow. "She wasn't violated, just roughed up, Caleb."

He held the man's knowing gaze. It wouldn't take much for the physician to understand Laurel's story about the soldiers and then riding to him for protection, he supposed.

"Thanks, Doc," Russ offered a hand to his friend. "What'da we owe ya'?"

Coyote shook his head. "We can settle up in town later, when you come by the office for that visit you keep missing."

Russ cursed. "Son of a...if it ain't him being my mother hen it's you."

Coyote chuckled, then turned to Caleb. "You can go sit with her but mind you let her rest."

He nodded and eased the door to his room open. Laurel lay with her eyes closed, a bandage across her brow. She looked fragile, but he knew better. She was tough as nails. Still, all he wanted to do was hold her in his arms and make it all right for her.

He bent to ease Jesse to the bed but the boy still held tight to him and whimpered. Ah, it was just as well. If the boy needed to be held all night, then that was the easy part. He kicked off his boots and sat gently on the bed, careful not to rustle the covers as he leaned against the headboard. It might be a long night but he wasn't leaving either one of them.

Laurel stirred and winced, touching her brow.

Caleb smoothed a hand across her hair, easing her hand back down.

"Caleb?" She opened her eyes.

"I'm here." He whispered. "You gave us a scare."

She nodded. Tears escaped her when she saw Jesse. "He's all right?"

"He's fine," he whispered. "Bravest boy I ever saw. Made it alone in the storm almost to the barn. Got a little bump to his head, but the doc said he's fine. Won't let me put him down but I don't mind even a little."

Laurel touched Jesse's thigh fighting tears. "I suppose a branch hit me…it's hard to remember but…Oh, Caleb…I'm sorry to come here and bring you trouble, but I was so frightened…those soldiers…"

Caleb took her hand. "Sheriff will handle them."

She shook her head, her voice cracking. "No one came to help me. The streets were empty and they shoved Jesse to the ground and I fought them and got away and all I could think was to ride here…to you."

Caleb took her hand. "It's best, you can rest here. I won't let no one hurt you again."

"Pink, is she safe?" she asked.

"Ssshhhh, she's all right, too. Ed's looking after her. Now rest. I'll be right here." He gave her hand a squeeze. "But I want you to consider staying at the ranch, you and Jesse for now."

She gave it a moment of thought. "If I've learned anything, I have learned to face my fears, and I need to go back to town for my work." She closed her eyes, though she gripped his hand tighter.

"Rest." It was best he didn't push her to answer now as she was injured and fragile when it came down to it. Gods, even battered and bruised she was as beautiful a woman as he'd ever seen, even now as she left him for more sleep.

He studied her slender hand in his. She wasn't dainty and porcelain like some of the finer ladies, even if she had at one time come from money. Her hands were strong and callused with short clean nails, he supposed which made her work easier.

Well, if she wasn't willing to come to the ranch, then he needed to teach her how to handle the pistol she owned or marry her one. The later idea was a bit more interesting and something he'd let play in his mind for a time now. He was busy, ranching taking most of his time, but of late and since meeting her, having a family of his own was something that felt more appealing than it had even a few years ago.

He studied her face. She was a strong woman. Beautiful and bold. A great mother and she knew horses. He wanted to touch her, hold her, but for now, she had her reasons of needing to prove who she was to herself, and he supposed he had to allow her that. Though without a doubt, he was certain with a bit of time and a little persuasion he'd find a way to make her his…if it was the last thing he ever did.

Chapter Five

Laurel sat in bed, eating broth with a spoon and allowing the widow and Leona to care for her, even though she was better. It had been way over a week that Doctor Sullivan had indicated she would need to rest, and she'd insisted Caleb return her and Jesse home after two nights in his bed. Talk in town was cheap and she needed to get back to her work, and she was still angry she'd gotten frightened enough to ride out in the storm endangering her and her son.

"Now dear, you finish up that soup." The widow tugged her blankets higher. "Gotta get your strength back and all."

"Yes, thank you." She lifted the spoon to consume the hearty liquid, knowing without a doubt the Widow Lowery would keep on until she finished, though she was growing tired of broth and honey bread.

Across the room Jesse played with his toys quietly. She had worried about him at first but he seemed his usual, only once mentioning "bad men gone, gone" of which she had reassured him they wouldn't return. But she still worried as his sleep was restless and he woke during the night crying which was unusual for him. But Leona had stayed at night to care for them both and had been a big help to allow her to heal.

Of course their care wasn't the same as being at the ranch with Caleb. He'd been attentive to her meals and cared for Jesse who had enjoyed all the animals. Caleb had all but insisted she stay at the ranch, but this was best. Back to her normal routine, though her heart still raced any time she thought of him and how tender he'd been.

She supposed she was better. The bruises to her face and thigh would take time to fade but she had no more pain. The widow cared for her on and off each day and Laurel caught herself wondering at times about the things she had not asked the elderly woman.

"Widow Lowery. Would it be an imposition that I ask of your husband and what happened?" She'd never asked before and Leona hadn't known much either.

Mrs. Lowery went about her work, folding a few linens and wiping the small table in Laurel's room. "Oh, I was married to Horace when I was a young girl, only fourteen. He was a merchant in Nebraska and asked my father for my hand and I suspect gave a sum of money to Papa. But I was smitten and the wedding was short but beautiful, even had pictures made. Horace had a pocket full of money, but he was nineteen years older than was I."

She glanced out the small window and continued. "We owned a mercantile or two and I did the sewing most often. But after we settled here, Horace began to fall ill on occasion. Doctor Sullivan said he suffered from heart dropsy and one day he just never woke up." Her voice never wavered as she spoke. "Oh, he was a handsome man in his day, though."

"And you never had children?" Laurel didn't want to overstep any of the boundaries, but the widow continued freely.

"No, I suppose the good lord just didn't have that

in the plans for us." The widow shook her head. "Though it weren't for much of a lack of trying." She cackled and Laurel stifled a giggle, though heat rose to her cheeks.

Widow Lowery continued tidying up and Laurel changed the subject. "Well, I should think that I've gotten the dress shop behind, so I'll begin again tomorrow and spend time here catching up the hand sewing to make sure we don't fall further behind."

The old woman turned, "Only if you are up to it, now mind you."

"I am sure I will be fine." Laurel took more of the broth. "I can rest evenings and I am no longer in any pain."

"Seems the men come through here rougher than when we had the Indians and all the fighting that took place years ago. I do wish that no-good sheriff would up and retire. We need a man in here who knows how to sheriff, get this town in order." Mrs. Lowery hissed as she worked.

"Well, he did get the two who attacked me turned over to the Cavalry, according to Mr. Holt," she responded, tearing a piece of bread. Caleb had come by to see her briefly one evening, wanting to check on her and Jesse. He'd let her know the men had been identified and turned in to the Cavalry captain. He'd also let her know had that not happened, he'd have dealt with them.

"That Mr. Holt's a temper, I find it hard to believe his care for you." Widow Lowery gave her a speculative glance. "Seems a might smitten with you, but you best keep your distance from a fighting man like that. His uncle is nothing but trouble, town drunk, needs a good jailin' if'n you ask me."

Laurel focused on her bread, taking small bites. "Well, he was very kind to rescue me from the worst that might have happened, and had he not found Jesse, well, I hesitate to think things might have been much worse."

"Yes, well, the sooner we get you back to work and busy, the sooner he won't have his worries of you." The widow eyed her and turned. "I'll be downstairs if ya' need anything."

"Thank you." Laurel watched as she left and then tossed back the covers, setting the broth aside. She smiled at Jesse who was scribbling chalk on his slate, occupied for the time being.

She inhaled a deep breath and got up, stretching and taking a peek out the sun-laced window. The town was busy and it had been several days since Caleb had come by, though he'd talked about following the herd with the black stallion once more. Maybe he was just to his work so she'd have the few days to heal.

Lands, she did remember his holding her the first night after the attack as she slept in his bed. Talking to her and easing her worries and fears. Somehow his touch had let her sleep. He was kind and he wanted to spend time with her, and she'd never afforded the idea of love once more in her life.

She'd never thought much about marriage again, thinking perhaps she wasn't at liberty for that freedom, and while Jonah had been gone for over a year, maybe it was that she could look to her own happiness after all.

Yet she'd never expected Caleb, with his deep brown eyes, tender words and honest love of her and her son to come to her but it had. She glanced at Jesse.

He deserved a father, a man to lead him to grow up. Caleb had already shown interest in teaching him, playing with him for hours as she had rested.

She moved to straighten the linens on her bed. Maybe she would allow herself to forget Jonah and give Caleb the chance to win her broken heart. After all, wasn't life so very short? Maybe with time, she would find a life with Caleb as she'd come to the conclusion that she already cared for him enough to think it was love she felt for him. Real love, the kind that didn't leave a woman and child in the dark.

****

Laurel rocked the pedal on the sewing machine, the heat of the afternoon catching up with her as she tried to create the dress one of the ladies in town had ordered. The pattern was from back east, but she hardly needed directions to follow it. She'd sewn the style dress before but the pink satin was fragile and required a tiny sewing needle and great care not to damage the material.

Leona had taken Jesse with her for a lunch break, and the bit of extra time would allow her to finish, with her son occupied and the widow out to her own shopping as she did sometimes at noon.

"Pretty, even as she sews." Caleb's large frame filled the doorway, startling Laurel from her work.

"Oh...you frightened me. What're you doing here?" Laurel's pulse bounded inside her chest at the unexpected sight of him. She stopped the sewing machine with her feet.

He stepped inside the small room where she did the sewing. "Had some business in town, sold a couple of mares and a colt. Wanted to check on you and Jesse again."

"We are well, thanks to you." She stood from the chair, straightening her skirt. He was incredibly handsome, enough so that it took her breath for a moment as he stepped even closer and without asking leaned to kiss her cheek and then her lips. She wanted to sigh but held her breath.

"Been waiting too many days for that." He touched her hair, tugging it behind her ear.

Heat warmed her face. "If the widow returns from her shopping, she'll take a broom to you for being in here."

He chuckled. "Is that right?"

"Oh, yes, she runs men out of here all the time if they come snooping. Unless they need mending or want to purchase a shirt or trousers, she takes that big broom of hers and sweeps them right outside the door." She smiled but he leaned in again for another tender kiss.

"Well, if I am going to get swept out of here, then best I make it worth it." He smiled, his face wearing a few day's stubble, which made her lips tingle all the more. "Besides, the widow likes me, she even smiled at me the last time I saw her."

Laurel struggled for words more. "Actually, she warned me of you. That she thought you smitten and I should stay busy with my work to avoid you."

He adjusted his hat. "I'll win her over, but maybe I should shave first. Been out for a few days, following that herd with The Black."

"The herd we saw has remained?" she questioned.

"Caught them a couple of days ago and rode to follow, but that Black is a smart one, disappears the herd every time, but he's in the area. Think I'll bring him in this time." His brown eyes showed his enthusiasm.

"You'll capture him then for selling?" She wondered how it was done here in the west with the wild herds.

He nodded with a lift of his brows. "He's eluded me a couple of times now. Hard to bring in a stallion that doesn't want to give up his freedom. If and when I catch him, he can add to the herd, got a pasture of mustangs, collecting a few at a time. Raise a small herd of those, but he'll gain me a good price on any foals he sires. Won't sell him though."

"Well, you'll be back out to him soon then. And I see the widow walking this way. That broom may have your name all over it, Mr. Holt." She smiled. "But I would ask if I'll see you on Sunday, it's Jesse's birthday as well. I'll have a cake, perhaps you'd join us for the celebration in the afternoon by the creek."

"Mr. Holt was my father and is my uncle." Caleb glanced out the window and quickly snagged another kiss, this a deep passionate kiss that left her knees weak and her body shivering. "I'll be there. And I'll be wanting another one of those when Jesse naps."

"Oh, you will?" Laurel's lips parted and her breath left her short and all she could do was nod as he disappeared outside onto the streets of Wylder.

She supposed he wasn't being forward given she'd given her permission of sorts, but she was no young girl and life had dealt her a bad set of cards. Her hope would be that what was growing between her and Caleb would be something of real love, though at times Jonah lingered in the back of her mind.

"Oh my lands, Laurel, he just kissed you." Leona

scampered inside, leading Jesse to his toys and letting go of his hand.

Laurel turned, her pulse still racing as she sat back to her machine. "Leona, you mustn't share that with anyone, at least for now, but yes he has kissed me, more than once."

Leona leaned closer, whispering as the widow returned inside going to the back. "Laurel, he's only one of the richest men in the territory and I reckon I ain't never seen a handsomer man. He kissed you... Laurel you may be able to get out of this...leave this filthy town and live in that big house of his and have more babies...oh and you'll be rich in love and horses."

"Leona, you must swear to me for now this will remain with us." Laurel lifted her gaze to the Widow Lowery who came in fanning herself.

"Hotter than a pile of potatoes on the pot out there." The widow glanced at Leona, "Back to work now with you both. Ms. Adams, the gown will need to be finished earlier than planned. I ran into Mrs. Carson and she's leaving town for that wedding she's going to a few days early."

Laurel nodded but gave a scolding glance to Leona who patted her chest and gave her a knowing grin.

"Yes, it will be ready at the latest by tomorrow at noon." Laurel made the promise but that also meant she might well be sewing in her room come evening and until late in the night, but at times the widow would pay her extra if the customer made any sort of tip. She began with the sewing machine once more, but the bobbin caught and the machine stopped with her lack of focus.

She took things apart and rethreaded the bobbin

and began once more. It wasn't the machine, it was her and her racing pulse, knowing Sunday couldn't come soon enough. Oh, she was much like a school girl in love once more in her life. She glanced out the small window and wiped her brow. Surely, she must have looked a mess to Caleb, but oh my, she had not expected a kiss or two here in town.

He'd been so handsome, with his tan trousers, heavy brown boots and a light long sleeve shirt with his bandana at his collar. He wore a hat like all the men in town, only his was a lighter brown felt with a string that allowed it to hang down his back when he wasn't wearing it. His face held a day's or more scruff and as she sewed, she licked her easily chafed lips.

It was true as Leona had said that he was wealthy. She'd had a good look at the ranch while there and the house was beautiful. It had windows that let her view the ranch as she recovered, and each room was neat and tidy for a single man living there, which was surprising.

But somehow this wasn't about money, at least to her it wasn't. Oh, money was nice and it made things easy, but she wanted what she'd been denied by Jonah when it came down to it. A home, a real home and a place to raise a family, though she'd pinch herself to wonder if she were dreaming that might come to be with Caleb Holt.

Chapter Six

Laurel woke from a deep sleep, reaching for Jesse who had begun to cry, gunfire blasting from somewhere in town, most likely the saloon. Since they'd been attacked, his sleep was more restless and he often woke startled by even the lesser sounds of town, just as did she.

"Shhhh…it's all right, Jesse." She cuddled him close to her and jumped as more gunshots blasted and the laughter of men on the streets echoed. She patted Jesse's back and it only took a moment for him to doze again, though for her that wasn't going to come. It was only a few hours until dawn and she got up, walking to the small window.

A soft knock at the door turned her.

"Laurel, it's me, Leona."

She eased the door open, allowing her friend inside. Leona had a room on the back side of Lowery's Dress Shoppe and it was even a mite smaller than her own.

"I heard Jesse cry, I thought maybe you were up." Leona stepped inside and sat at the table. She wasn't complaining, though, about her small room as it held her bed which she shared with Jesse, her trunk and the one chair with a small table. And of course the wardrobe with her clothing and Jesse's.

"He's already sleeping again." Laurel sat on the

edge of the bed covering a yawn with her hand.

"Those rowdies out there are up to no good again." Leona followed her yawn, her dark hair hanging loose around her shoulders, and her nightdress covered with her coat. "I brought cookies, made a batch last night. Come on, take ya' one."

Laurel reached for one of the cookies, her stomach letting her know it was empty with a hinting growl. "Thank you, Leona."

"Sheriff just run them all off, like he can do much more than try these days." Leona talked with her mouth full of the treat. "Guess it won't be long at all 'til Widow starts barking her orders...the water's too hot, this one's still stained and these need to lay flat to dry..."

Laurel shrugged. "I believe she means well, she's just set in the way she prefers things." Leona was right, but Laurel would never complain as if it weren't for the widow, then how would she and Jesse have survived.

"I suppose. Been thinkin' 'bout what ya' said, where you could teach me to sew as good as you." Leona lifted her brows. "I can sew a button and stitch a hem, but ain't good at all in knowing the way of that machine you use."

She shook her head. "I could teach you a bit each day on our lunch break and you'd know a lot in a few weeks. It's the least I can do for you minding Jesse while I was recovering."

"Oh, he's such a joy to care for." Leona glanced at Jesse and back to her. "Always thought maybe I'd have a few of my own one day, but as it is, never married."

Laurel studied her. She was probably around the same age, in her early twenties, yet she knew very little of the wash woman's story. "Leona, you are such a pretty woman, I should think one day you will find the right man. How was it you got here to Wylder anyway?" Well, the younger woman could be pretty but as it was, she dressed in men's trousers and long shirts most often and her hair was simply pulled back in her floppy hat all the time.

"Came with my Pa several years back, but Pa caught the fever and died almost as quickly as we got here. I's a girl sixteen and only thing I could do was the wash. Worked for the widow since then, keep my room with what she pays me, but ain't never much met any man it seems. Reckon I'm just not so pretty to the men, raised by my Pa since I's little and all."

"Well," Laurel stood, "come here." She brightened the lamp a bit and sat Leona's chair by the mirror on her table, lifting her brush to run through her friend's messy hair.

"What're ya wanting me to do?" Leona seemed uncomfortable eyeing herself in the mirror.

"I'm going to smooth your hair, show you just how beautiful you really are," Laurel answered, running the brush through her hair and lifting sections to swirl a bit of curl around her fingers. As she did, she pinned her hair into ringlets. She had beautiful dark hair and amazing amber eyes, but it wasn't like she knew that about herself.

When she was done and Leona was staring at herself in the mirror, she went to her wardrobe and pulled out one of the dresses she'd sewn a while back at the mining camp. It was too small for her to wear any longer since having Jesse.

"Here, stand up and let's try this on." Laurel waited

as she stood shaking her head. "Never wore one so fancy as this since I's a little girl."

"Well, if you like this one, I am giving it to you." She waited as Leona removed her coat and let her night dress fall, leaving her naked.

She put the bottom of the fancy pink satin down over her friend's head and let it fall, adjusting the ties in the back and tugging the sleeves into place. "I can take it in a little but look at how really beautiful you are."

"I don't know if I've much seen myself in a mirror of late, but I am so pretty." Her friend remained quiet for a long moment. "Oh, but Laurel, I can't accept this…it must've been so expensive and all."

"Nonsense, I sewed this one myself and it no longer fits me since I had Jesse." She smiled. "It's yours now."

"I am pretty ain't I?" Leona beamed with pride.

"Of course you are." She hugged Leona. "And I'll teach you how to take this in and sew the next one."

"You really thinkin' I could do it?" Her friend's happiness was contagious. "I mean I'm fast at learning and all but a little unsure."

"Oh, sure you can learn, but it will take commitment and practice." She picked up her cookie again and took another bite. "Though you might have an easier time of selling cookies. These are scrumptious."

"My Ma's old recipe. She was the best cook, though she died when I's near ten." Leona took another for herself with a chuckle. "I'll save my cooking for myself, mostly don't care to do it, much like the wash, but if I could sew like you, the widow might pay me more and I could make myself a few more nice clothes with your teaching. Yours are so pretty and all, look at you, even your night dress is a fancy one."

"Well, I…" She touched her white linen gown, sewn with tiny pearls at the edge of a ruffled open neck, "I have been sewing for a long time, since I was a girl. It does take years of practice."

Leona angled a hard look at her. "You're better now, will ya be goin' back out to the stream? Maybe see Mr. Holt again?"

She glanced back at Jesse who rolled over in his sleep, and thought on it. "I think so, but would like to keep that between us, not for the widow." She had missed Caleb, who had come by a few times, but not stayed long with the widow lurking nearby.

Her friend eyed her with speculation. "I think Mr. Holt might be smitten with the likes of you with him a grabbing those kisses I seen."

"Well, the widow has warned me of him." Laurel brushed aside the idea. "He's been so kind to me and Jesse."

"Mr. Holt's a temper when it comes to them there horses he raises, likely be how he is if'n he had a family. He beat up a man here years ago enough to almost kill him and when he fell on you, he was in a fight. They say his uncle and father came out here long before the war and started selling horses after they fought off the Cheyenne and Sioux. He's not so much like the other men around here, staying in the Social Club, never see him a-goin' in there."

It had been several days since Caleb had come by the dress shop, and she'd been planning for Jesse's birthday at the stream. "Well he's been very kind, but I shall watch myself and make sure his intentions are good ones."

"Well, ya asking me and ain't no man up to too much good intentions when it comes to being smitten to a woman. My Papa warned me a man ain't a wantin' but one thing and that I should marry him before I let that happen. Though I ain't a-knowin' much about that at all." She nodded and glanced at herself again and at the clock on the wall. "Gonna go get the fire started under the pots, might be the widow squawking at me if it ain't hot enough this morning. But gonna run to my room and hang this up so it won't get dirty. Oh, thank you." Leona hugged her and then was gone.

She got up to close the door behind her and returned to bed, pulling the quilt over her and Jesse, though she was certain she would get little more rest. At least the town had quieted, just leaving her an hour or so to rest before beginning her morning.

She turned to her side and dimmed the candle, gazing into the flame, thinking of Caleb. The kiss between them had happened quick, and maybe she'd been too fast to agree to spending time with him, but she'd never expected his coming to her rescue either, as if some sort of fate had placed him there at the right time. She supposed she shouldn't have fallen so easily into his arms and to the sweetness of his words in wanting time with her. He was a kind man, wasn't he, though she was married? At least on paper.

She'd loved Jonah and she supposed that was why his leaving her and Jesse had come as such an utter shock. But he'd changed over time, caught up in his quest for gold, and rarely in camp. Oh, he'd always been tender and sweet with her, trying to convince her that he'd make a claim and find gold eventually, but even their marriage bed had become less than fulfilling. Jonah returning after a day's dig and riding her hard for the few minutes it took him to finish, with no thought to her pleasures as he'd always seen to in the first months of their marriage.

They'd met young, at a party held by one of her father's friends. Jonah had asked permission to court her. She'd known then his aspirations of heading west to land for the taking and she'd fallen right into the belief a new life was to be found farther west. So was the thinking of a young woman with ambitions of running a homestead alongside her man. And while she'd thought of returning home to Tennessee when she'd found herself alone, she had no real family to speak of there; and her father's home had been sold on his death. It seemed Jonah had left her little in the way of choices with leaving her for his quest.

She turned again in the blankets and closed her eyes. Morning was coming and while the work was hard and her lack of sleep often left her exhausted, it was only two more days until Sunday and a chance to visit the creek and perhaps see Caleb Holt once more.

****

Caleb urged Jericho to a full gallop, the herd of mustangs with The Black stirring up dust before him. He'd been on them a time or two the last few hours and he had his eye on the stallion. The large horse was as black as midnight bearing a fully blond mane and tail. He wasn't fond of taking more than the yearlings out of the herds, but this stallion had eluded him more than a few times.

He spotted the horse and leaned forward, gripping the rope. Maybe this time. The Black knew him, as more than once they'd sparred off out on the western pass where the open land fed into forever across the plains. He held his thighs tight, the length of the lasso held in his mouth as he gripped the hoop in his left hand.

The stallion turned the herd which had shied of him and Jericho as it was, but he held their flank and the horse in his site.

"Today's the day, Black, reining you in for the catch." He said it through his teeth clenched on the rope. "Need some of that fight in my own herd and you've a couple of stallions waiting to take your place, old man." He gave a chuckle. This could end well or not, but he was taking the horse home this day.

Jericho held steady, picking up speed and holding true to his name, bred for endurance if nothing more, though the stallion held the pace of the wild, the untouched wild beast faster.

The wind hissed in Caleb's ears and his hat fell away from his head, the strap catching at his neck as it fell across his back.

He caught a pace as the stallion turned the herd ahead once more, and watched as they all moved as one, the terrain of grasses and sand making Caleb pull the bandana from his neck over his mouth and nose, squinting his eyes as he held the animal's gaze. The Black knew and so did he that it was today, it was now, and he eased the lasso into position.

Seconds passed, the drumming of hooves, the wind in his ears, the heat of the sun and he and the horse began the dance of this game they had played more than once. And then there was silence as Caleb found the hesitation in the stallion and sent the rope ahead, letting go with his hand and mouth as he kept the end of the line and held Jericho steady. The whip sounded in a slap as dust took Caleb's gaze and the rope caught in his gloved hand.

The Black reared as the herd bypassed him into the distance and Caleb slowed Jericho, adding tension to the rope. He'd done it, the stallion snorted and tugged hard at his capture, rearing and fighting with a strength Caleb couldn't hold for long. He stopped Jericho and wound the rope around the saddle horn and dismounted, keeping a grip to the length of the rope as the horse snorted and hissed his capture against Caleb's triumph.

He'd have to let the horse do his cadence in no longer remaining free, and while he wanted to cheer this moment, something inside him wore the same pain as The Black. He'd been born wild, free to run and free to fight for the herd he'd claimed. And for the moment watching The Black fight, Caleb allowed the horse more rope, hearing his father's voice.

Break the horse, not his spirit, Son. Tame the beast, not the animal. Feed the Spirit of the animal and you'll own him even if you set him free.

Sweat ran down Caleb's back as he held the rope and eased himself closer to The Black inch by inch, holding the animal's dark eyes. "Easy…you knew it was me…and you knew this day would come." He spoke in a calm but breathless voice.

The horse reared as he got closer and Caleb gave a bit of rope, stepping back and allowing the horse his measure for another chance to fight. His heart raced and the sun bore down, the air filled with the dust as Caleb held tight.

The stallion gave a shrill cry of defeat, his blond

mane lifting and distinct against the animal's dark coat.

Let him make his peace when you take a stallion, or you'll never have his respect, Son.

Maybe it had been years now since he'd heard his father's voice, the man who had taught him to know horses, having never laid a hand on him or an animal and certainly never his mother.

The thought brought him to Laurel as he played the dance with the horse. The last few weeks she was the first thought he'd held each morning and the last prior to giving up to sleep. The recent kiss with her at the stream had met him with surprise on how she hadn't resisted and had even agreed to him seeing her again. He'd taken more kisses at the dress shop. And he wasn't sure at all he would be any good at some kind of courting, other than just spending time. But hell, a woman wanted flowers and nice things, and it seemed maybe it had been a long time since Laurel had had those things.

The Black reared again, kicking his front legs in the fight. The herd had moved on, leaving him behind. He was no longer fighting for their protection as doing so to free himself. This would be a hell of a horse to break when he got him back to the ranch.

He moved in again. "Easy…easy now. That wild heart of yours about done?"

The horse stopped, his dark eyes unblinking in wait. Caleb stood still for a long moment and after a time took a step closer and then another. The horse shied, giving a loud snort. "That's it, gonna touch you here in a minute. You know me."

He took another step and lifted his right hand slow and sure and placed it on the animal's side, The Black watching him and trying to rear again though he held the rope. He touched once more and the horse tensed but didn't move. "That's it. We've been at this a couple of years now."

He held The Black's gaze as he stepped back and gave a gentle tug to the rope. The stallion made the step and then another, having eased into understanding his capture and following Caleb another few steps. This went on for several hours and until The Black settled, sniffing at the wind as he mounted up on Jericho heading to the ranch, leaving him to wonder if his triumph was worth yielding the horse from the only world he knew.

Chapter Seven

Russ walked up and leaned on the corral fencing, shaking his head. "How the hell d'ya do that?" His uncle gave a chuckle. "Figured you'd followed the herd to bring him in."

Caleb nodded, keeping eye contact with The Black he'd put in the high corral the night before. "The western slope last night, the herd's still hanging there. Sent Cane and Ed to nab a few mares."

Russ gave a laughing grunt. "Calm him with the ladies he knows. Never thought the stallion would be taken. You'll be the talk of town, but if anyone could've got 'im, you did it, boy."

The horse made a run full around the corral as Caleb moved closer. Looking for escape and rearing, the stallion having calmed little over night. It'd take days of this to even be able to touch the animal again, if the corral could even keep the creature fenced. Caleb fathomed he'd had a sleepless night, worried the horse would break his borders, yet it was Laurel who occupied his mind most often.

Caleb walked over to his uncle. "Don't seem the ladies ever calmed you much. Ed mentioned he saw you heading out of the Social Club again. Guess I don't have to ask if you came home on a drunk with a near broke back."

Russ cursed. "As a matter of fact I didn't come

home drunk, but I don't need you watching my back, like the damn mother hen you are."

Caleb grinned. "Then Miss Adelaide must've had customers, sending you home." The madam ran a tight ship and didn't tolerate Russ on a drunk. She most often put him to bed alone and kicked him out in the morning.

"You know, instead of minding my business, it's Sunday, how 'bout you make your way to the creek and see 'bout making an honest man out of yourself with that pretty seamstress?" Russ put on the challenge.

Caleb shoved his hands to his hips. "I told you it's not like that, at least not yet."

His uncle cackled, his thick gray mustache moving as he talked. "Then make it like that. 'Bout time you settled down. Get yourself hitched where you can dip your wick on a regular basis and you'll find you're a new man."

Caleb turned back to the horse. His uncle had never been worth a damn at holding his tongue. The man could and would say anything. "It's complicated, I don't know…"

"If'n she don't scare the hell right out of you, then likely she isn't the one." Russ lifted his gray brows in challenge. "Aw, now, I'm just funnin' ya a bit." He adjusted his hat. "You getting up to near thirty, time you thought about settling, raising some boys to pick up the work around here. I ain't gonna be able to help forever ya' know."

"Not if you don't lay off the bottle." Caleb turned back to him, The Black moving to escape his approach. "And I turned thirty already."

Russ's brows furrowed. "Thirty already, well then

damn time you drug your happy little ass down to the creek and win her heart one sweet nothing at a time. Pick some flowers along the way. The ladies like that sort of thing. You got it in ya', somewhere underneath that hard ass your father put into you. Why'd ya' think I never moved in that big-time house with you? A family belongs there. Trust me, she'll be the best thing you never planned."

Caleb looked on as Russ walked away. He hadn't known that, though his uncle was right about his father. Rick Holt had been the more serious brother of the two. He'd worked Caleb hard to learn the ranch and with his schooling growing up, and for that he'd helped the ranch stay successful, the various breeds and wild herds keeping them in business for years now.

He cursed under his breath, looked once more as Russ disappeared back inside the bunkhouse. He could be overbearing, but he was right and it wasn't like he hadn't been thinking about Laurel every second of every damn day. It was nearing noon and it was Sunday and The Black needed a break and for that matter so did he.

****

Laurel waited as Caleb spread the quilt on the ground at the stream. She'd ridden out later than usual and Jesse had fallen asleep for his afternoon nap on the ride. Caleb had helped her down from Pink and grabbed the blanket making things easier.

Nearby Pink grazed, her tail swishing in the slight breeze that was a relief from the scorching heat.

Her morning had been spent making a small cake with icing for Jesse's birthday and a nice meal of stew and bread which she'd kneaded earlier that morning.

When Jesse woke, she'd let him help with icing the cake as well as kneading the bread. It was hard to believe he was three now.

"Birthday boy's fast asleep." Caleb spoke in a soft whisper lifting the picnic basket she'd had tied to the back of Pink. The ride had taken longer as well in trying not to let the horse run and make a mess of it all.

"You remembered." She lay Jesse on his side on the blanket, though he never stirred. He was wearing a new shirt she'd sewn for him and his new boots which he'd insisted on sleeping in since they'd been purchased.

He spoke as he sat the basket beside her. "Of course, turning three is a milestone, a big boy now. Waited but thought maybe you weren't coming."

She sat as Caleb did the same, keeping his boots off the blanket. "I'm afraid I had a lot of help today with the meal and making a cake and then Pink wanted to run, had to keep her from taking off not to spill the stew."

He leaned in and kissed her cheek. "Laurel, I wish you'd reconsider staying here at the ranch. I mean I have plenty of room for you and Jesse both. And he can play here and you can ride Pink. We'll get to know each other better spending time."

Laurel shook her head. "It sounds wonderful but the widow would never allow it. I need my work and have pushed hard for me to make a way for me and Jesse. It isn't that I don't appreciate what you offer but...I think it's best I stay in town to keep my work."

"Town's just not a good place for a woman alone," he rebutted, watching her sort items from the basket.

"We're fine really, though Jesse's been restless at

nights since the attack. But I wouldn't have town thinking I'm a kept woman, Caleb."

He glanced to where her son lay sleeping. "He uh…is about as tough as you walking through that storm. He was crying hysterically but he did it. Brave as hell."

Laurel rested a palm on her son's back. "I appreciate your wanting to protect us both and I do want more time with you, Caleb. But the proper way, not where we give town a reason to gossip."

"Wait here, got something for you." He trotted back to Jericho for the wildflowers he'd collected earlier. He had tied them with a bit of rope but they were nice. Small orange flowers, the stems as green as Laurel's eyes. He held them out to her. "For you."

She took them as he sat once more. "Oh, they are beautiful."

"Thought maybe for the birthday you needed something nice, too." He leaned in to kiss her, slow and tender, making her want to swoon as a young girl.

"Told you I was gonna want another of those." He held her gaze, a palm on her cheek but shook his head. "I, uh…got another surprise for you if you're willing." He angled his head and went on. "If you're feeling up to it, maybe I could watch Jesse for a bit and let you take Pink for a ride, a real run through the pastures. Give you some time to spend with her."

"I don't know. He's been so clingy." Laurel looked at Jesse and back to him. It wasn't a bad idea as long as Jesse didn't fuss of it.

"Come on I'll keep a good eye on him. Brought a small pole to teach him to fish." He glanced back at where he'd tied off Jericho.

"I would so love to ride Pink where she could gallop hard. All right if he's agreeable." Laurel glanced at the horse, having not been able to ride alone very far when she did.

It was then Jesse began to stir, lifting his head, glancing around and giving a whimper.

"Well, good afternoon." Laurel lifted him and kissed him as she pulled him into her lap.

"Eat cake, Mama?" He spied Caleb and his eyes lit up with a grin curling his lips. "Papa, eat cake, too."

Laurel froze for the moment and glanced at Caleb who held her son in his sights. She supposed the many stories she'd read to Jesse each night had taught him about mamas and papas and maybe this had been bound to happen.

Caleb's brows lifted and lowered but he held her gaze the same. "How about you and I go fishing while Mama rides Pink for a little while?"

It wasn't hard for Laurel to know Caleb had quickly changed the subject as neither of them had known the response.

"Go fishing, Mama?" Jesse looked at her and back as he stood pointing to the stream.

"It sounds like fun, catching fish." Laurel got up and waited as Caleb trotted to Jericho and returned with the small fishing pole, Jesse forgetting all about the cake.

"This here pole I had when I was small, caught a bunch of fish on this one back then." He unraveled a bit of line. "But it's got a hook and it hurts if you touch it."

Jesse tucked his hands behind his back but followed as Caleb went to the stream and used his knife to dig into the dirt. Jesse looked back at her with a big grin as Caleb lifted a couple of night crawlers and added them to the hook.

"Now, toss her in." He handed the small pole to Jesse who held tight with both hands as Laurel looked on.

Caleb let go of the pole. "Hold tight and when it pulls, you'll have a trout on there."

Jesse stepped closer to the stream, waiting but then the pole bent and he tried to hand it back to Caleb.

"No, sir, pull him in, it's a fish, back up and pull." Caleb instructed and a few steps later, Jesse lifted the pole, a small trout dangling.

"Fish!" Jesse gave a shrill scream. "Mama, fishing."

"My but you sure have a big one on there." Laurel's voice rose an octave at her son's happiness. "We'll have trout for supper then for your birthday."

Her son giggled and watched as Caleb removed the trout from the hook and held it out to him. "Here ya' go."

The toddler shook his head, hiding his hands again.

"Come on, now, if you catch him you have to hold him up to show him off. He don't bite." Caleb waited as Jesse found the courage to take the creature by the mouth.

The boy turned to show her the fish. "Fish, Mama. Jesse fish."

"Oh my, it's as big as you." Laurel bent to Jesse. "Can you stay here and catch another while Mama rides Pink for a little while?"

He studied her. "Mama come back?"

"Of course, Mama will ride for a little while right here while you catch another fish." She tried to sound convincing.

He grabbed the pole again. "Worms."

Caleb gave her a nod and she stepped away toward Pink as he talked to Jesse. "You dig for a worm, careful and all. The knife is sharp."

Laurel made it to Pink, glancing back as her son lifted another fish from the water with a giggle. She mounted up, urging the horse ahead. She'd had little time for this, time to ride free as she'd once done growing up. She'd ridden for hours then, along the pastures and trails of home and as she took Pink to a swift gallop, she was once again like that girl, innocent and free.

The wind found her, muffling her ears, and the mare moved even faster, aware she was able to give a good run. Laurel bent and tasted the wind, letting the summer sun warm her back as Pink ran farther and farther from the stream. She inhaled a deep breath and urged the horse to fly. "Go girl."

And Pink understood, moving as if the wind herself, allowing Laurel's mind to clear and her heart to know, this was the life she wanted. She could easily love Caleb as she had no one, especially watching him with Jesse and how tender he had been with her as she recovered. Maybe he was right in that no one here really cared she was married. Maybe she would simply toss her caution aside for the chance at something as real as spending time with Caleb, and maybe, just maybe she would open herself to the idea of love once more.

Chapter Eight

Thunder hinted in the distance, heavy dark clouds moving across the sky and stealing the sunlight from the evening.

"I suppose we should head back to beat the rain." Laurel glanced behind her and back to Caleb as they sat at the stream.

He looked at the clouds overhead and over the rise, "It's still a ways off." He held out his hand and drew her closer. She moved with ease and settled in beside him.

She glanced at their joined fingers. "Jesse loved the wooden animals you carved for him, he's needed some new things to play with."

He glanced at Jesse, who held both wooden horses even as he slept. He'd had spent a couple of weeks working on the details to make one look like Pink and the other like The Black, painting them both. And the boy had remembered, holding the small black horse and pointing in the distance where he'd seen the stallion.

Caleb gripped her hands, noting the strength and her lack of resistance at being in his arms. He placed his lips to hers and eased her to open, their tongues dancing until she sighed. He still clung to her hand, but used his other to remove his hat, laying her back on the quilt.

"Now's the time you should smack me if you're not liking this." He touched her cheek, taking her mouth once more before she could protest.

She was so easy to kiss, open and active in giving him the same. He moved his mouth to her cheeks and her neck and placed a hand underneath her breast and ran it the full length to her hip.

"Am I moving too quickly?" he whispered when she tensed.

It was a moment before she answered as she tangled her hands into his hair. "No."

"Laurel, I see the bit of fear in your eyes, but you don't need it." He touched her cheek. God, he wanted to part her legs and move hard inside her, until she cried in pleasure, but he would follow her lead. "I'm not those men in town, and I'm not Jonah, who'll leave you behind. I want something real, Laurel, but I don't want to rush you."

"You are so kind to me and Jesse. I know and I want this, all of it with you, without worrying about being married any longer but I still do." She explained what he understood well enough.

"It's been a year, Laurel, it's not looking like he'll return." He shook his head and touched her hair as thunder rumbled above them and the wind lifted.

"You're not gonna have time to get back to town, come on, we'll ride to the house." He took her hand and helped her up. "You can see The Black."

Her mouth fell open. "You brought him in? Caleb, why didn't you tell me?"

"Too busy taking in the scenery." He kissed her cheek once more as they sat up.

She quickly packed her bag and the food items into the basket. "Of course I'd love to see him, but this storm may catch us and I've had enough of storms lately."

"We'll beat it back. The Black's none too happy, gonna take some time to get that one broke." He glanced at the horizon and the coming rain, miles off across the pastures.

"We'll hurry." He waited as big drops of rain began to fall around them.

She stole a quick glance behind her at Jesse as Caleb grabbed her bag and the basket tying them to Jericho and bringing both horses almost to the quilt. "We don't want to be an imposition."

"You can't get back in this. Too dangerous and it's lightning in the distance toward town." He nodded and she turned, ducking as thunder rumbled closer. "Wrap Jesse in the quilt and I'll take 'im. Didn't think this one was coming on so fast, or maybe I was distracted."

She began with Jesse as he held Pink for her. She handed Jesse off to him and he placed him over his shoulder as she mounted up and then he turned to do the same, making it look easy even with carrying her son.

The rain picked up and he adjusted the hat on his head, "Just follow, we'll ride right into the barn."

He glanced back, taking Jericho to a canter making sure she could follow, but then after watching her ride Pink all afternoon, he had nothing to teach her about her skills. He'd been caught up in how she rode into the wind and turned the horse and even how she had Pink jump a set of fallen trees. He had to admit he held his breath for that second but Pink had cleared them and made off on a continued gallop, with Laurel handling the landing with ease. Well, it was worth watching her in those pants if nothing more. Not many woman in

Wylder wore pants as she did most Sundays.

But holding Jesse across his shoulder, the boy still unmoving, he hugged a bit tighter. Teaching him to fish today had been a bit of fun he hadn't taken for himself in a long time. And though it had been awkward at the boy calling him Papa, there was some part of him that hoped he heard those words more often.

He urged Jericho ahead and into the open doors of the barn, dismounting as Laurel rode Pink in behind him.

"Lands, I've never seen a storm come that quickly, well at least until this one and the last." She shivered as she dismounted, her blouse wet and her hair hanging free and dripping of rain. So beautiful, though it seemed maybe she didn't even know how much so.

He shook the water from himself and took his hat off, placing it on her. "There's no one inside. Russ is off to Denver for a horse and the boys are out, probably taking cover elsewhere. I'll get you to the house and then come back to brush down the horses." He handed her Jesse. "Leastwise, you can see The Black later on."

She gave a nod and bundled her son in her arms.

He held them at the barn doors as thunder clapped and lightning zapped all around them. Nothing about this storm that was letting up. "Ready?"

She took off as did he, running for the house in the solid downpour that was cold as ice. He kicked open the door and shook himself of the water, caught off guard at her laughter.

"Your hair is as soaked as mine now." She brushed the hair back from her face as she took his hat off and put it back onto his head, holding Jesse over her shoulder.

"It's a good one, gonna go get the horses settled, be back in a bit. There's drying cloths and blankets inside, just find what you need. It'll take me a bit." He adjusted his hat and headed back to the barn in the heavy downpour. He shivered from the cold of the rain, shocking the heat right out of his skin.

He made short work of removing the saddles from both horses, brushing them down and stalling them all while The Black kicked and stamped his resistance in the furthest stall. Caleb walked that way which agitated the horse once more.

The mustang snorted and gave another buck. "It's all right, you'll get used to things little by little." It would take the animal months to accept to his voice and him as a rider, but it was hard to shake the feeling he had in taking a stallion from the herd. No matter the years he'd done it, it had never been easy and for some reason with The Black, it didn't feel the victory he'd thought it might. Maybe The Black wasn't made for capture.

He turned and made his way outside the barn, closing the big doors, and making another run for the house. Inside, he sat his hat aside and kicked from his boots in the mud room and stepped through to the main room of the house glancing around for Laurel. He tossed another couple of logs on the hearth fire and stoked the flames back to glowing. The large firepit would have the house warmed in no time, but he didn't want her or Jesse to take a chill.

He moved down the hallway, spotting Jesse covered in the small bed he'd had as a youth and turned to enter his own room and stopped short—forgetting his next breath.

Across the room at his dresser, Laurel used a cloth to dry her hair, which flowed fully down her back into wisps of bouncing brown curls. She had taken the pins out and sat them in a neat pile and she was wearing one of his shirts.

She caught his gaze in the mirror but didn't try to cover herself as he'd thought she might, her purpose rather clear.

He glanced away, uncertain of anything more than his inability to breathe. "I, uh…the horses are good, gave them oats but the storm's a pretty bad one." He wanted to look at her body, wrapped in his oversize shirt, but out of respect kept his eyes down.

She spoke then, turning. "I put Jesse in the bed across the hall if that's all right. I'm sure he'll sleep until morning."

He nodded. "Yeah, that's…that's, uh…fine." Damn but he stuttered all over trying to speak.

"And I borrowed your shirt…" She turned, unmoving as she stood before him. The storm shook the house, or was that the beating of his damn heart at the beauty of her?

He moved to her, slow and sure, and reached for the towel in her hands and touched her hair. She held him with those sweet green eyes and it didn't seem as though words were needed as she leaned into his embrace. He inhaled the sweet scent of her damp hair and she wrapped her arms around his middle.

He held her back from him. Damn his want of her was fierce, but she had to be sure. "Laurel, you don't have to…"

She touched his lips and then placed her fingers to the buttons of the shirt she wore. "It's time for me to let go of the past, love you as I've wished."

Caleb stopped her, placing his hands with hers. "Only if you are certain, because once won't ever be enough, Laurel, and I'll want you to become my wife."

"I want nothing more, Caleb," she whispered, her breath short.

He bent and kissed her plump lips until they parted. He teased her mouth, though her replying kisses were more urgent than his own. She devoured him, her hands going to the buttons of his shirt once more which he simply tugged over his head and off, followed by his undershirt, both finding the floor. For a woman uncertain moments ago, she now touched his chest by flattening her palms to him and moaning as he took her mouth once more.

He let his hand rise slowly, easing it underneath the shirt until he cupped a breast. He squeezed with enough pressure to make her sigh. Damn, she was as near to perfection as he'd ever held but then she gave a hard shiver.

"Want me to stop?" he offered, though if she denied this between them now…

She held him with those deep green eyes for a breath of seconds, her breath short. "No…"

That did it. He lifted her into his arms and plopped her on the bed, making short work of his trousers and long underwear. He was aware of her gaze on him as he joined her on the bed.

She shivered again as he laid open the shirt, bearing her breasts, and the soft patch of curls between her thighs. He touched her cheek and let his hand slide lower to her breast again, running a palm across the soft bud until it pebbled under his touch. He bent his head and tasted the other with a tender lick followed by a suckle and her chest lifted with her soft wanting sigh.

Thunder sounded, shaking the house, and the rain continued to pound in droves across the tin roof.

Caleb tasted the second nipple, teasing with a series of hard licks and suckles and her breath came hard. She let her hands run down his sides and back up to his chest, massaging the hard muscles there.

Thunder crashed and lightning filled the room with a flash as he let his hand slide down her belly to her center, easing his fingers to the tiny pearl of her pleasure.

Her lips parted and her hips moved as he began the slow circles, the tender touching that would make her reach the climax he wanted for her. He teased her mouth and her cheeks and went back to her breasts, as he eased his fingers inside her.

She stiffened and gave a loud sigh. "It's been so long for me…"

"It's all right…" he whispered as he moved deeper with each stroke. There was something about her slight British accent that made him love her voice. "Just me and you, Laurel."

Her hips moved with him and several moans left her as he continued. She lay in his open shirt, her eyes half-glazed and her breath coming in short pants.

He kissed her partially open mouth, whispering. "Just me and you…"

"Caleb…I want you…" She tensed and he obliged, removing his fingers from her and pushing her legs apart, filling her in one swift hard stroke that made him groan in satisfaction.

Laurel moved with him as they began the slow

dance of give and take, her hands kneading his sides at his ribs and her knees riding his hips. He lay fully on her, rocking in motion to meet her and relishing how easy it was to love her, their bodies fitting as one of perfection.

Laurel sighed against his shoulder, nipping at his skin, her hips moving, urging him ahead. He lifted himself, thrusting deeper, her continued sighs filling his ears as he made each impact into her body. And as she tightened around him, she gave a stifled cry of his name.

"Caleb…"

He rocked into her with earnest, watching her face distort as the pleasure took her, her nails digging into his shoulders as she gave a series of soft cries. And only when she stilled did Caleb give into his own desire, pinning her and roaring through the thunder of his own hard release.

****

The curtain at the open window moved with the light wind following the storm. A chill eased across Caleb's skin, making it prickle as he fought to catch his breath. He eased from Laurel and curled in behind her, holding her to keep her close. She was perfection and he'd never be the same man again after making love to her.

"Caleb…" she whispered as thunder continued to fill the night.

"Huh…" He kissed her shoulder inhaling the wildflower scent of her hair that was still damp.

"I never loved him as I do you," she whispered, though he was sure she had tears given the break in her voice. "I loved him and some parts of me still do, but…my heart is so full of you."

What was he to say to that? He'd fallen in love with her overnight but he had no reservations about it at all and he would make her his wife as soon as they could work out the details. "You don't deserve those tears and my hopes are I never bring any of those to you unless they are for happy reasons."

"I wasn't ready to fall in love ever again, but then there was you…and I never expected love to come so easily." She quickly wiped her cheeks.

"I think maybe it comes a lot easier when you find the right one. But this pleasure here, touching you, that's only part of it, Laurel. That pleasure is ours alone on rainy nights, afternoons by the stream, evenings right here. Me holding you until your pleasure is complete." He hugged her closer to him, knowing he'd go to the ends of the earth to make sure he saw her smile each and every day. "But more than that. I'll be here, Laurel. I'll always be here if you want me to be. Hold you when you hurt or when you're sad and when you're happy and as you laugh and while we play with Jesse. All of it."

"Where did you learn to love so fully with that heart of yours, Caleb Holt?" she whispered lifting his hand to kiss his fingers.

"Never loved until you." He was certain he hadn't.

"I wish to be your wife, Caleb, but I still worry about my marriage." She turned to look at him.

He wrapped both of his arms around her and kissed her shoulder. "We'll give it some time, but I want you here at the ranch where you and Jesse can go to the stream for him to play and for you to ride Pink in the pastures any time you wish."

"But my work?" She frowned.

"You can keep your work, bring that sewing machine right here and do the work here and return it," he said. "As long as you get the sewing done, why would it be any different?"

"I suppose, but if we aren't married and I stay here…" She shook her head.

"Laurel, town's gonna gossip no matter, but once we're married it'll fade fast." He reassured her, though he supposed it was a concern for a woman. "I want you and Jesse safe and back to the kind of life you both deserve."

"Caleb…"

"Huh…"

"Love me once more this night." She turned back to face him and kissed his lips, tugging him to her and arching toward him.

"Well then, bring on the damn thunder." Caleb pulled her atop him and tasted her mouth once more, reckoning round two might simply do him in once and for all.

Chapter Nine

Laurel woke to the bright sun warming her face, uncertain for a moment where she was. She glanced around the room. Caleb's room and she was still naked in his bed, the storm long gone. Lands, what had she done? Her boldness in allowing his touch had been a surprise to even her, but she had no doubts of her love for him. But given the morning sun, she was sure she'd slept for far too long. She jumped from the bed and donned her clothing from the night before, which had been folded neatly and lay over a chair, now dry.

Jesse would be awake by now, but then she heard their voices. Her son and Caleb, along with another she didn't recognize, and laughter, that included Jesse's voice.

She glanced into the mirror and ran her fingers through her hair, though she hadn't a brush, and pulled it back using the pins she'd left on the dresser the night before. Facing herself in the mirror, she gave a hesitant smile. She was certainly in love now. Lying with Caleb complicated things, but it seemed her heart held a lightness she hadn't known it could.

And then she noted the wildflowers in a small vase that hadn't been there the night before. Caleb again. She touched the open petals and smiled, though more laughter from down the hall turned her. She glanced at the clock on the wall, it was nine o'clock. She rarely slept this late. She opened the door and made her way down the hallway she'd come down the night before, wishing she had fresh clothing.

She stopped in the doorway of the big kitchen, admiring her son's laughter as he held, of all things, a baby chicken.

"Jesse got two big fish." Jesse held the chick in one hand and used the other to show how big the fish had been to Caleb and the other man, who she assumed to be his uncle.

"Uncle Russ, Jesse caught two big fish, bigger than the ones I caught and we fried them up for breakfast this morning." Caleb eyed her, waiting.

Russ chuckled and tousled Jesse's hair. "Well, that's a big deal for a boy, his first fish and darn near bigger than you." Russ noticed her with a nod. "Morning, ma'am, didn't see ya' standing there. Russ Holt nodded.

Heat rushed to Laurel's cheeks with the fact he probably understood she'd been in Caleb's bed all night. "She nodded. Good morning, please call me Laurel."

"Mama." Jesse jumped from the chair and ran to her to show her the chick. "See, Harold. Baby Rooster."

"Oh, my, a baby chicken named Harold?" She admired the small captive. "Be gentle with him."

"Join us for trout for breakfast. Jesse's a fine fisherman and Caleb knows how to cook 'em." Russ pulled out a chair and nodded. He had shoulder length gray hair and a thick mustache with at least a day or two of beard growth, but his eyes were very much like Caleb's.

The thought of fish sounded scrumptious as her

belly gave a grumble. "Thank you." She glanced at Caleb as he sat once more and placed a trout on her plate along with a scoop of potatoes and onions.

"Jesse's fish, Mama. Eat." Her son eyed her plate as she tasted the fish.

"Yes, and they are so very good." Actually the bit of the fish was flavored so well with spices she couldn't say it was fish as it tasted more as chicken. "My compliments to the chef."

"He does know how to cook for sure." Russ continued with his own meal, it surprising her he used a napkin.

"It was you who taught me." Caleb kept his sights on her.

Laurel focused on her food, finding it a bit awkward with his uncle present, but the man stood after shoving a heaping spoonful of potatoes into his mouth. He chewed and swallowed hard. "How 'bout I take this fisherman to see the goats and pigs?"

Laurel looked from him to Caleb but Jesse jumped down from his chair and followed. "Go see goats and pigs, Mama. Bye."

Laurel lifted her brows at Jesse's eagerness. "Well…I suppose…that's all right."

"Ahh, he'll be fine, the men are here, the storm hit a bit of the bunkhouse and they're making repairs. Russ, you don't mind?" Caleb glanced at them both.

"Jesse go, Mama." He took Russ's hand, holding Harold against his body with the other. "Uncle Russ."

Laurel nodded. "All right then, you mind your manners."

The elder man chuckled. "Got six goats and one of the nannies had twins. Come on boy, me and you gotta feed all the animals around here. You two go on about your day."

Laurel watched them go to the door and disappear outside. "I don't want him to be much trouble."

Caleb turned her, pulling her into his embrace. "He'll be fine, Russ loves kids, he raised me, didn't he?"

Laurel shook her head. "Lands, your uncle here, he must know what we…well, what we did…what…" She cringed, closing her eyes and shaking her head as she opened them again. "The flowers were nice."

He took her mouth in a deep satisfying kiss that took her breath. "He won't say a word. Besides, he told me I needed to settle down with the likes of you a while back. Come on and I'll let you see The Black and I'll get the horses saddled for a ride. Me and you got something to see today."

"But I haven't any clean clothing and my hair must look just awful and the widow will have my hide." A moment of panic hit her and she flitted to move away from him. "I must get back to town."

He grabbed her. "It's all right. I had Cade run to town early and he let the widow know the storm caught you and you were feeling poorly, caught a chill."

"A lie, Mr. Holt," she teased, though a smile slipped as she mocked.

"A silly white lie, but after last night, I want a little time with you more. Show you The Black, a place I like to ride to and I'll get you and Jesse back to town this afternoon, and smooth things over with the widow."

Laurel gave a nod and he led her to the door and outside.

"Leastwise the widow was understanding, worried

about you catching your death and all." He laughed. "I think Cade made sure she understood him to be our chaperone."

"Well, when she gets you with that broom you will wish you rushed me right back to town late last night, even in the storm." She shook her head as they stepped to the corral where The Black was pacing the muddy ground.

He was so very dark with a white mane that appeared almost silver. "Isn't he beautiful up close, but none too happy still."

"Took me two hours of working him to get him to follow Jericho back. He's got a wild heart when it comes down to it." Caleb leaned on the fencing. "He's not showing any idea he's gonna take to this, though, and maybe I should have known that."

"Breaking a horse like him would be very dangerous I suppose." She stepped back as The Black stamped his feet and snorted.

"Not gonna rush it. He has to get used to the corral and me feeding him, touching him." He held her gaze touching her hand. "Kind of like someone else I know."

A blush heated Laurel's cheeks. "I'm not a horse."

He chuckled and wrapped his arms around her from behind. "That, woman, I know good and well given your own wild heart. But tell me, did I do all right, last night?"

"Seriously, Caleb." Her face heated.

"Well, it's been a while for me, and you said the same, want to make sure I did things to please you." He chuckled and she gave him a shove and he changed the subject. "Brought Jesse out here this morning to see The Black. His eyes were as big as saucers."

"Well, he adores all animals. He'll be as happy with the goats and pigs to my guess, but now Harold...I'm guessing Jesse won't give him back up." At best she figured the chick was now part of the family.

"Harold was kinda smaller than the others that hatched, so Russ let Jesse have him. He...called me Papa again. Won't tell you I didn't gloat a bit." He beamed.

She let that sink in for a moment, uncertain but saying what she had to anyway. "I suppose all the stories I read to him where there are mothers and fathers but...he doesn't remember Jonah and has never asked."

He nodded. "Come on, got something I need to show you, like I said. It's not far."

He saddled Pink and Jericho and then he helped her to mount up. She took Pink to a canter following his lead, relishing in another ride, but worried a bit about the white lie to the widow and the fact she was still married. But as it was, some part of her mind had let that go and she was not going to look back as she became Caleb's wife. The one place she truly knew she wanted to be. His love of her and Jesse was like living a dream come true and so as she'd told herself, she was hanging on tight for it all.

****

Laurel dismounted, her mouth open in wonder at the valley below which was filled with horses and high cliffs in the distance, where she could see as far as forever. "Caleb, this is absolutely breathtaking."

They'd ridden for several miles and he hadn't said a word, though he walked up behind her, Jericho's reins in his hand. "My Pa and Russ purchased this back before the war, why I pride myself on the horses and the business we've built. It's one of my favorite places."

"And all the horses are yours?" She asked.

"Yep, most raised here, some of the mares we keep here until they are in season." He stepped closer to her.

"Well, it's maybe the most beautiful place I've ever seen." She turned a full circle and then back to the canyon, admiring it all.

"Wanted you to see it first, before I gave you…" He reached into his trouser pocket and lifted a small velvet pouch.

Her heart skipped a complete beat and then raced inside her chest. Was he…? Oh, Lands…was he going to propose for real? Her mouth dropped once more as Caleb loosened the ribbons and reached inside, struggling to pull out what was there.

"I suppose I am a bit of nerves, but only because I ain't much a man of words and all." Satisfied he bent to a knee. "But I want to do this right by you. Laurel, marry me, and let's watch Jesse grow up here and let me spend every day putting a smile to your happiness, say yes?"

The pounding in Laurel's chest was audible and without reserve she gave him her answer, sealing her life to happiness she'd never thought she would find again. "Yes…Caleb."

He tilted his hat back and took her hand and slid a ring on her finger.

"Wait, wrong one." She giggled and handed him the other hand.

"Hell, I don't care what finger you wear it on…"

He pushed the ring to fit, a gold band with a single tiny stone of green at its center. He stood again and tugged her in for a kiss. "Last night was really special, but I want to know you're mine and I want to do right by you and Jesse like I said."

"Caleb, it's really beautiful." She'd never seen such a ring and it did fit her finger perfectly.

"I made it. The stone's from one of my mother's necklaces, and when I thought of a ring for you, the stone is just the color of your eyes." He'd used the gold from another of his mother's rings, reshaping it and adding the tiny stone. "It's called Jade, from Asia, China, somewhere like that."

"Oh, Caleb, last night…" The heat rushed her cheeks as he pulled her into his embrace. He'd made love to her more than once and she'd never known the deep pleasure he'd brought to her, the sweet release of her love that was for him.

He chuckled.

She pouted. "You make light of me, it had been a very long time for me."

He shook his head. "Not making light of you, never held anything as beautiful as you, Laurel, but…best we get things planned, you could be…preg…"

She placed her finger to his lips. "Perhaps we shouldn't think of that now, but…I'll have so many things to plan. The widow will be upset, I suppose."

"As well as you sew, she will let you work from the ranch. I got a buggy in the barn, you and Jesse can ride into town to drop off and pick up your sewing like I said," he suggested as she leaned closer. "No need to stress the details today. I know you like your work and I'd want you to keep it."

Pink nosed over to her, pushing at her side in search of sugar. She laughed. "I'm afraid no treats right now, later girl."

He gave the animal a pat, and she moseyed along munching the high grass. He turned Laurel, stepping in behind her and wrapping his arms around her, kissing her neck. "And one day, Jesse will have all this to call his own and I can teach him the land and horses. He was so damn proud of those fish."

She giggled again. "You are so good to him…and me."

He whispered at her ear. "And on our wedding night, I wanna bring you here. Make love all night long, watch the stars move across the sky with you in my arms."

"You are bad, Caleb Holt," she whispered, covering her grin with the back of her hand. "And I feel your desire against my backside."

"Well, now that's just what you do to me, woman." He turned her and kissed her again.

She pulled back. "You make me very happy, something I thought might never come again, Caleb."

He held her then for a long moment, giving her heart a warmth it had been so long without and she clung to him as if he were the sole reason that allowed her breath. And as it was, she inhaled as deeply as she could.

Chapter Ten

"Come on. No one's around for miles." Caleb took Laurel's hand. "Seein' you own a pistol, it's about time you learned to use it. He paced off into the high grass, dragging her along.

She followed, lagging a bit, not at all excited to shoot the weapon. It was late Saturday evening and she'd ridden out on Pink with Jesse as soon as she'd been done at the dress shop, Leona the only one she'd told about Caleb's proposal.

Her friend had been more than excited for her, but she'd let Leona know she wouldn't be moving out to the ranch until they were wed, though she was well aware coming out to the ranch on a Saturday evening was Caleb's way of making sure she'd stay the night. Smoothing things over with the widow the week before had gone well but she didn't want to have to do that again.

And Caleb's idea to teach her about shooting the pistol was because she had not agreed to stay at the ranch until they were married. He was anxious to do that right away, but she wanted a bit of time to plan things, sew a new dress, and she'd ordered a pair of boots out of Chicago that had cost her twice as much as Jesse's.

"I know I need to learn but I do not wish to kill any animals." She tried to suck down her fears as he stopped and turned back around.

"Ah, best you not worry about animals but all those no goods in town." He checked the bullets in the pistol and glanced ahead of them. See the old log by the tree. There where the trunk is upturned. The mark there where it's rotted."

He raised his arm, squinted an eye, and the gun blasted, making Laurel grab her ears and duck. "Nothing to it but a steady hand. Here." He handed her the gun. "Biggest thing is keeping it cleaned and well oiled. Otherwise if might backfire your way."

She held the heavy gun, glad they had left Jesse back at the house with Russ. Feeling the weight of the gun once more she wanted to cringe. "The last time I pulled this out I was about to shoot you."

"You never cocked it, remember?" He stepped in behind her and held her arm steady, whispering in her ear as he placed his hand over hers to cock the weapon. "Every gun is different. One eye and put the target dead center of the small cutout."

She gripped the gun and squinted an eye, focusing to do what he said. Lands, she wanted no part of this, though having him so close to her…how on earth was she to focus steady?

"All right." He waited, saying nothing more.

Laurel braced and pulled the trigger. The blast hit near the mark, though her nerves wanted to shatter.

"Not bad. Again." Caleb checked the gun and handed it back to her. "Aim's off a little, ease it left a bit."

"Yes, now that I'm partially deaf in both ears." She focused again, anticipating the click of the hammer and the blast.

He chuckled from behind her and the rumble of his deep voice penetrated her body.

She did her best once more, taking a deep breath and firing. The mark he wanted her to hit blasted apart. Her mouth dropped open and she swung around, still gripping the gun. "Did you see that? Lands, I hit right where you told me."

"Whoa." He grabbed her hand and turned the gun away from him. "Respect the gun, aim at no one."

"Oh." Laurel handed the gun back to him. "Sorry."

"Look, the thing is,"—he checked the weapon once more—"when you pulled the gun on me, I wasn't too worried because you hadn't cocked it. But if you aim to use a gun, cock it as you lift it."

He handed the pistol to her and stepped back. "Don't move." He drew his revolver from the holster and in a rapid succession fired the weapon six times. She covered her ears again. When he stopped, she lifted her gaze and the mark they'd been aiming for was gone.

"Well, I suppose I'll never be as good as that." She shook her head and wrapped the gun and stuffed it back into her bag. "Though I keep it put away mostly so Jesse doesn't get his hands on it."

He nodded. "I'll teach him one day when he's older."

"As your father taught you?" She asked.

"Him and Russ both," he remarked as they headed back to the horses. "Russ didn't come back to the ranch until my mother died when I was twelve. He and my father had fallen out of sorts and I guess when she was gone, he felt he could return."

"Why?" She asked.

"Ah, neither have ever said it but they fought over

my mother. I guess Pa won the fight, so Russ left, but when he did return, it was like nothing had happened." He glanced at her and back to where he'd fired and shrugged. "It was kind of like having two Pa's I guess."

"Well, it seems he did a fine job along with your father of raising you, and Jesse has grown to adore you both. I worry, Russ might not wish to see so much of the chickens and goats." She relished in him taking her hand as they moved toward the horses. "And lands, but Harold has begun following Jesse everywhere when we are at the ranch."

"Russ has always liked the little ones." He let go and handed her Pink's reins. "I'm kinda partial to Jesse's mama, though."

She mounted up, her heart full as he turned and climbed up onto Jericho. He led the way but she allowed Pink to catch up to his horse. "I told Leona of us, of your proposal, but I haven't told the widow yet."

"I think the widow will come around, maybe hint at the dress you said you started." He beamed. "Can't wait to see it on you and make you mine."

She nodded. "I still worry, Caleb, about the fact I am married…and what may be thought of me. Some in town know Jonah left us and all the gossip…"

"Laurel, you've no marriage, not when he left you like he did and hasn't returned. And now my bed's been empty for a week. Don't like it much that way." He was stern with the remark.

She grinned as he took Jericho to a light gallop. "You are very bad, Caleb Holt. Perhaps yours is the wilder heart."

He only chuckled and glanced back at her. "Yes, ma'am, I'll take that as a compliment."

Laurel's mouth fell open but she stifled a laugh allowing Pink the run and speeding ahead of him, turning back with the lift of her brows in challenge as he followed with a loud chuckle.

****

"He's sleeping, finally." Laurel eased the door closed to the small room where she had lain her son. "He was so excited to see The Black again."

Caleb nodded, stoking the fire and turning to her. "The Black's complicated for now. Not sure what I'm gonna do."

She moved toward him, as he frowned. "What do you mean?"

"Ahh, some part of me hunted that damn horse for way too long. I guess I thought when I caught him, it would be as easy as all the others over the years, that maybe I'd relish in defeating him, but it's not like that. Maybe I had no right to take him when it came down to it, as he'd beaten me several times before." He sat on the settee, kicking his feet up to the small table there as she sat beside him, leaning into his shoulder.

"I thought getting him reined in would be something special, but I don't think this horse is meant to be broke. He's been wild for a long time and I feel a bit guilty in taking him from all he was. Proud. Strong."

"What will you do?"

His voice vibrated through her and it seemed she could listen to him for hours and never tire of his words.

"Russ says only I can decide." He shook his head. "Laurel, I've lassoed stallions for years now, most I've trained to be good saddle horses, but the Black. He's smart, he looks at me and he knows I feel this way.

111

He's settled little, because ours had been a dance of back and forth for a couple of years. Gonna turn him loose here in a bit."

"You think he cannot be broken?" She asked.

"Oh, he can be broken, but my father always told me when you break an animal, don't break his spirit and to settle The Black down….well, I'd break more than his spirit, I think." He'd already decided what he needed to do.

"But if you turn him loose, won't others pursue him?" She shrugged.

"No one except me has ever come close. They all talk about him, but no one's ever done it." He put both hands on his knees. "I saw the herd, still hanging around where I nabbed him. Lost without his lead. Even the other younger males are too afraid to take his spot."

"I suppose I understand your returning him, but your business and selling horses, isn't it what you do?" She had no real idea of how things were done with the ranch.

"The Black's different. His heart is truly wild…it's time I took him home." He stared into the fire as he spoke in a whisper.

"Maybe that's why I love you so, your ability to find the fairness in all things." She tilted her head, her deep green eyes, holding him as tight as if her hands were on him.

Caleb turned and placed his lips to hers. "You think this is good then."

"I think if your feelings are such that it bothers you this much, then the decision is the right one." She tasted his next kiss. "But when will you release him?"

"Not sure yet…" He kissed her again. This time

easing her lips to part and tease. "Wanna not talk anymore about the horse?"

"Sounds like a fine idea." Her pulse raced. She'd thought of this on and off all week.

"Good." He began to undress her, starting with the buttons of her blouse.

"Here?" she asked. Though the window held draperies, Russ or one of the hands could enter the house.

He chuckled. "Russ is down for the count, Jesse tired him out and the boys are in town. Looks like it's just you and me."

Laurel smiled. as he continued with the buttons and then cursed with her stays.

"Let me." She eased from her shirt and then pulled the clips of the stays close together until the bodice opened fully, heat touching her cheeks.

"Rather nifty." He inspected the garment. "What happened to the ties?"

She whispered. "I'm a seamstress, ties can take too long."

"Won't miss that trick next time." He growled and stood up, pulling off his vest and shirt and then bending between her knees. "Never told you how much I like a woman in pants. Makes it easier for you to ride and for me to imagine."

She giggled as he tugged first one boot and then the other from her feet, setting them aside. He eased her stockings off and tugged at the pants, and in one swift movement had them off her, leaving her in her chemise and her pantaloons, the thin ones made to wear with her pants. He lifted her to sit on the couch again and fitted himself in between her thighs as he kissed her neck and down her chest, across her chemise, tasting a nipple through the fabric, leaving it damp.

Laurel couldn't help the sigh that left her as he teased her nipples outside the cotton garment. Lands, but before when he'd made love to her she'd climaxed so quickly she hadn't been sure of her own body's response. She'd found pleasure with Jonah at times when he was patient with her, but it had taken her little to cross over with Caleb's touch. She closed her eyes, letting him be all there was as he teased again through the fabric.

And then she gasped as the warmth of his mouth found her bare nipple, drawing tender and then harder, her chemise gone and her pantaloons drawn lower. Oh, but she needed Caleb where she ached. Where she wanted the hard breech of him to shear her and take her to the pleasure. She moaned as he put a hand on her chest and eased her to lean back on the settee, still partially sitting.

He opened her legs with an eager grin and ducked his head. Laurel sucked in a deep breath, wanting all he'd give her to bring the pleasure she desired. What she'd done without for so long. Was it wrong to want this, even his mouth on her time and again, teasing. She moved with him as he closed his lips on the pert nub of her pleasure. Oh dear, she wanted to hiss, to open further for him, so he'd have all of her. She moaned…and moved her hips, squeezing her nails into his shoulders as he increased his pace, lapping and sucking.

And as he had before, he read her body and moved with her as she crested, her body drawing tight and the spasms of sweet release finding her, making her rock as he tasted more and more of her and until she held him back with her palm to his cheek.

She closed her eyes. Surely, this was a sin of God, to want what he'd done and still want more, but so help her she did. "Lands, Caleb…"

He joined her on the oversized settee, filling her in a single stroke of his hips, her tender body yielding, though she tensed. The stretch of him surprised her once again though her body took him fully. And she began to move, holding him as they worked to become one.

"Thought of nothing but this all week, holding you, being deep inside," he whispered, and she imagined she blushed, but then the fire was rather warm and her body was feeling him again, edging toward the pleasure. She ran her hands along the muscles of his hard shoulders, kneading the strength there.

"Yes," she managed but then he eased from her and the settee and tossed a pillow to the floor, urging her to her knees with her body across the cushions. He moved in behind her and she gasped as he pressed inside her again, her entire body giving an uncontrolled shudder.

"Ahh…" She gasped as his fingers touched the nub once more, adding pressure.

"Easy now…" He upped his pace, nudging her legs farther apart, allowing him deep access within her.

She gasped with each impact of his body into her, glancing over her shoulder at him. He held his eyes closed, pumping into her, satisfaction holding on his face. He was beautiful, all naked and hard in want of her. She pressed back into him and he groaned, picking up his pace until her breath was short and her body tightened again. She gripped the pillows as she came, with Caleb finally tossing his head back in a loud roar of pleasure, filling her one last stroke that he held deep as his large body jerked in the heated spasms.

Caleb eased them to the thick rug and pulled her to him, kissing her hair, heaving to catch his breath. He lay behind her and tucked her hair from her face. "I love you, Laurel."

She turned and cuddled into him, taking his face with a hand on each of his cheeks and pulled him to her lips, kissing him on the mouth and then each cheek and holding his gaze. "My heart will always be yours…"

Chapter Eleven

Caleb watched the herd come in closer, The Black sniffing in the wind and wanting to rear. Nearby, Laurel held Jesse, both having come with him to the creek to wait on the right time to turn the stallion back to the wild, the only conclusion he could fathom that was right for the stallion.

Sweat trickled down his back, and The Black held his gaze a moment longer. He wanted his freedom, but not without making sure Caleb understood he'd won after all. Caleb gave him a nod. "You smell 'em, well, I'm gonna let you go, boy. Gonna let you go back to the freedom you taste, because it's only right, but we'll call it a truce of sorts."

Part of Caleb's gut clenched and part of him knew it to be right. He glanced at Laurel and she gave him a nod. "It's the right thing, Caleb, he wants to be free again. Papa's gonna let Black go back to his family," she explained to Jesse who whimpered.

"Black, go bye-bye." The little boy chattered, reaching his hands in grips to try and reach the horse. "No, Black."

Caleb approach the stallion who gave a snorting buck. "Hold still and you'll be free."

The Black pranced away and Caleb followed and loosened the noose from his neck, but the horse pulled and it tightened. "Whoa…whoa now. If you want your freedom you gotta cooperate."

The stallion snorted and then sniffed the wind again. He had to wonder if the horse understood, if the animal knew he'd run free without the rope. He gave The Black another hard glare and the horse held still and in that brief second, he eased the noose from the animal.

The Black bolted, stirring up dust in his wake as he made his way to the herd which startled but circled around to the stallion. They hadn't forgotten him, lost until now.

Caleb watched as the horse reared on his hind legs and joined the herd, looking back as if in some kind of forgiveness if he was guessing right.

Laurel walked to him and put Jesse down. "He wanted to be free, Caleb, he belongs here. A bittersweet victory for him. Are you all right?"

He nodded, watching the stallion lead the herd to a gallop.

Jesse began to run. "No, Black. Come back." Caleb trotted after him and bent to a knee, holding the little boy to his chest.

"The Black needs his family. He's the papa and he has to go home to take care of the mamas and babies." Caleb hadn't expected the boy's tears and tried to explain as Laurel bent to them both.

"Want Black." Jesse held his black wooden horse and looked at Caleb. "Black is the papa?"

"Yes, he's the papa and they need him and he needs them." Caleb appeased the boy, who looked back at the herd as he held Laurel's tear-filled eyes. "We'll see The Black again when you're a little bigger."

Caleb stood again, helping Laurel back to her feet

and lifting Jesse. He studied the stallion in the distance. The magnificent horse reared in triumph once more.

Laurel leaned into him. "He told you good-bye."

"Farewell." Caleb whispered. He'd done what was best and somehow could hear his father's voice of approval in the wind.

****

Laurel stood from the sewing machine and picked up a skirt that needed a lace hem added. She laid it on the board and used the heated iron to smooth the linen garment back and forth, the warmth of the shop overbearing once more.

"Good Lord, but the heat out there today might be a boilin' me outside the pot." Leona came inside sipping a tin of water and handed one to Laurel. "Here, drink, went to the well, it's cool."

She set the iron aside and took the other tin mug "It's indeed hot today."

"Oh Laurel, your weddin' dress is going to be so beautiful, maybe the most beautiful I've ever seen." Leona admired the dress she'd been adding to each evening once her duties at the dress shop were complete.

She glanced at the dress. It was simple but she'd added tiny stitches and fitted it to her size only days before. "It will have a bit of satin and lace layers across the bodice."

"Well, maybe if you continue to teach me, when I one day need a weddin' dress I will sew my own." The wash woman shook her head and admired the dress further.

"You are doing very well with the new dress we've started for you." She was proud of how serious her friend had taken to learning to sew.

Leona chugged the rest of her cup, burped loudly and placed a hand over her mouth with a smile.

"Leona." She scolded, having been working daily with teaching Leona how to act and speak like a woman. "Only to wear such a pretty dress you must act the lady who lives in it."

Leona nodded. "Pardon me."

"Better."

"Well if'n you ask me, you marrying Mr. Holt is about as romantic a thing I've ever heard of. First, he falls right on top of ya' and then steals that kiss and the rest is history." The young woman beamed, reminding her of her own happy butterflies that rode inside her from time to time.

"Well, I ironed out the details with the widow Lowery this morning." She had dreaded asking the widow about her taking her sewing to the ranch and returning things a day before their deadline.

Leona stepped closer, glancing at Jesse who slept in the corner. "She gonna get that broom of hers after you or Mr. Holt?"

"She actually said it would be fine for me to take the mending and sewing to the ranch as long as I return things on time. She was very accepting of it, actually happy Caleb approves of me still keeping the job." She had been surprised at the widow's support.

Leona eyed her with skepticism, "Likely she's just worried about the money she'll lose if'n you ain't working here."

"Aren't," Laurel corrected.

"Ain't, Aren't…" Leona scoffed. "What's the difference it makes, but yes'm."

"Perhaps, but you told me you had a couple of suitors when you wore your new dress to church, so I'm thinking you should hold your shoulders high and speak like a woman of means," she reminded her friend.

"Well, none of the two of them interested has come 'round, but they were a'lookin'." She frowned. "But I'm a gonna wear it again this week and do my hair up like you taught me with that hot iron. But for now, it's quittin' time. Too hot to work a might more."

Laurel went back to her work. It was good to see her friend learning how to be a woman and happy at trying.

The widow entered the shop. "Quittin' time is right, but you two girls clean up a bit and go on. Oh, but Miss Adams, would you run the finished dress from this morning to Eliza Jane at the Social Club?"

Laurel stared at the elderly woman for a long moment. "Sure, it would be no problem."

"Well, it's early yet, likely to be quiet there this time of day," the widow added.

Laurel nodded. She continued to be cautious in moving around town, but it was time she rose above the attack and didn't worry so. After all, she'd been to market several times now and things had been fine, that and she supposed word of her and Caleb had been whispered about.

She fixed up her sewing counter and set the hot iron to iron matting to cool.

Leona walked closer. "I'll watch Jesse for a bit while you run, let him sleep. I've a new batch of cookies in my room and when he wakes, we'll get him a treat and then bring him back to you."

"I suppose that would be fine, thank you, Leona."

Laurel gave her a swift hug and picked up the hanging dress and raced out the side door toward the Wylder Social Club. Town was as busy as usual but she made a short walk of it.

It wasn't like the business there was advertised, but the Wylder Social Club was, in short, a brothel. Most women in town stayed clear of the ladies who worked there though it seemed the madam and her daughter were highly thought of in town. Truthfully, she'd found conversations with Eliza Jane, who was from back east, of interest.

She inhaled a deep breath, and carrying the fancy dress, climbed the steps and went inside the establishment.

"Hello, Laurel." The tall, slender redhead was in the front room, sitting at the small desk there, talking with Aofie, the woman who cooked for the social club. She stood and took the dress.

"I finished it earlier today." Laurel smiled and accepted the slight hug from Eliza Jane.

Eliza admired the dress and hung it behind her. "I'll try it again later on. I thank you for the hard work on it. It's just beautiful, but I understand you are working on another dress each day…one in white?"

Laurel hadn't known that she was aware of her pending marriage to Caleb.

"Oh, your secret is safe with me, but Leona let it slip and the widow has passed the word at church." Eliza touched Laurel's arm. "Caleb is a very nice man and I know you'll be happy. Coyote has known him for years now and thinks highly of him."

She nodded. The two men were friendly and Caleb often talked of the doctor as well. "Thank you, he is a wonderful man, very kind and he adores Jesse."

Eliza Jane continued. "Oh my, he's just as adorable a boy as I've ever seen."

"Laurel had to agree. "Please, I won't keep you from your work. I need to get back to Jesse anyway. If you find the dress needs further sizing, just let me know."

"Thank you again and congratulations." Eliza Jane smiled as Laurel turned to go.

Walking back to the dress shop, Laurel caught herself smiling. It was all right that Eliza knew her not-so-public news, but as it was, she was still trying to keep things quiet until she and Caleb had set a date.

She eased up the stairs to her home and went inside, setting her purse aside and thinking what she might plan for her and Jesse for supper.

A knock at the door turned her and she sat aside the small bag of flour she had lifted, assuming Leona had returned with Jesse earlier than planned.

"Leona did someone wake already…?" She swung open the door and all she knew in the world came crashing down.

****

"Hello, Laurel." Jonah removed his hat, his blue eyes scanning her face and a hesitant smile easing across his lips as he leaned to kiss her cheek.

Laurel struggled to inhale a single breath, uncertain her legs would keep her standing, shocked, unthinking, numb. Words eluded her as she finally uttered his name, her heart racing so hard inside her chest she was sure she might pass out. "Jonah…"

He stepped inside, smiling as if a year had not passed them by. "Took me a bit to find you, but after a couple of towns, thought I'd try Wylder. No one at the camp could tell me where you'd gone, though they've moved camp farther north it seems." His voice was soft and he was dressed in fine clothing, his face with a well-trimmed beard and his hair cut short, something she'd never seen.

Laurel inhaled a ragged breath, her heart simply unraveling itself at his presence.

"Aren't you going to say anything, Laurel?" He looked down and stepped a bit closer and leaned to kiss her cheek again. "I missed you so much, you and Jesse both."

"What are you doing here, Jonah?" She forced herself to speak, the effort difficult.

He fumbled with the hat in his hands, his dark hair falling free across his brow. "I suppose I startled you but Laurel, but I struck, found a big vein of gold in the Dakotas and…I have money, Laurel, real money. For us."

She could no longer support herself upright, images of Caleb riding through her thoughts along with the confusion of Jonah standing before her. She wanted to scream or maybe cry, hug him or hit him, but was she dreaming or was he really here? She sat on the bed, folding her hands, the shock flowing through her visceral.

He stepped closer and took the chair across from her, nodding as if for permission. "I've come back for you and Jesse. Where is he?" Jonah glanced around the small room and back to her. "He must be running all over and talking by now, missed so much but now I can give you both a good life, Laurel."

And for all the prayers and hopes he would one day

return, Laurel fought nausea at what this now meant. He'd returned for them. How could she go? How could she stay? What of Caleb?

"Jonah…you left us and you didn't come back," she whispered. He couldn't think any amount of money would forgive what he'd done in leaving them the way he had.

He shook his head, frowning. "No, I left a note for you. I couldn't take you and the boy where I was going. I had to grab the spot heading to the Dakotas or lose it. I told you it would be a while before I returned and for you to move with the camp, but when I didn't find you there, I started going to town after town, for months now."

"There was no letter, Jonah, nor money. You left me and your son alone in the wilderness to find our way here." Her voice rose an octave as she tried to comprehend that he'd planned for her and Jesse after all.

"Laurel, I left both explaining, left you with the horse and…I expected you had plenty to make it. I was coming back for you both. You must believe me." He spoke, taking her hand in his. "I hadn't any time to explain other than to go or I would have lost the option to have a spot on the dig."

Laurel's heart pounding and the beginning of tears found her in the confusion. "You left nothing, Jonah."

He shook his head, glancing away. "Then someone took them while you slept, another in camp who saw us riding out. Laurel, you have to know I was coming back for you and Jesse."

"Jonah, you left me with a child, a horse, a sewing machine and a tent. I waited a week and then realized you weren't coming back." She fought her emotions and continued. "And I rode Pink into this town and found a way to feed myself and my son and my horse. You can't know how it was for me to prove myself and worry of your return that never came like so many things, Jonah."

"Laurel, I did this for us. We have money now. Real money, thousands." He pleaded, giving her hand a squeeze. "God, you are as beautiful as my dreams all this time." He embraced her and in spite of it all, she gave into his touch for a short time. Was it relief that he was alive? Or his return? She shook her head in confusion and pushed him back.

He held her gaze for a long moment. "I love you Laurel and I love my son. We have more money than you or I ever thought possible." He reached into the jacket of his fine coat and pulled out a small square piece of paper and unfolded it. "I've purchased twenty acres in the Dakota Territory for a homestead. A real home, Laurel, where we can be a family again...you and me and Jesse."

Laurel looked down where he grasped her hand and back up, unable to find any more words. But what of Caleb and her planning of a wedding and the boots she'd ordered out of Chicago?

"Laurel, I know you're shocked to see me but I was coming back and you have to believe that." He held both her hands together between his, the large hands that had once held her, loved her.

"Jonah, it's summer. Jesse and I have been here for months...alone and having no idea of your whereabouts," she scolded.

"It took me a while to find you." He shook his

head. "Like I said. I sent wires to town after town, not thinking you would have come as far as Wylder. I never meant for you to struggle so."

Laurel shook her head. None of this made any sense. Her heart raced, her mind whirled. Leona would be back with Jesse shortly and her son wouldn't know his father…the father who had abandoned him. The man who had abandoned her, leaving her to find a way to survive.

Jonah stood as if he read her mind. "Look, I didn't come here expecting quick forgiveness, Laurel. Haven't done a lot of things right in this life and the worst of that being you and Jesse. But when I hit, all I could think about was finding you and doing my best to make things right once more. I know you need a bit to think on things, but the train leaves for the Dakotas next week and I want you and Jesse to come with me. Give me that chance Laurel, please. You're my wife, Laurel, and Jesse's my son and I want us together again." He begged, his head shaking but his deep blue eyes holding her hostage.

Laurel remained uncertain of her choices or any answers, so shocked she wasn't sure of each breath she was taking in.

He turned a full circle. "I never meant to hurt you but I knew I'd hit, I knew I could make it for us, Laurel. I've a room at the hotel. We'll talk again tomorrow when you've had time to think things over. But you and Jesse deserve better than all this and now I can give you that and we can get to know each other again and I can get to know Jesse. He's well?"

"Yes, he's fine." What could she say to him? Jonah might have been guilty of his fever for gold, but he had come back, even after almost a year's time he was here now and suddenly her choices as a woman were clear. She was still his wife.

"Look, I've a meeting tonight but come to the hotel in the morning and I can explain more and we can talk about things." He moved out the door shutting it behind him and leaving her to her thoughts which wouldn't settle.

Leona popped through the door, holding Jesse by the hand. Laurel glanced up unsure how much time had passed since Jonah had shut the door.

"Mama." Jesse ran to her and hugged her around the legs and then went to his toys in the corner.

Leona shut the door. "Laurel, ain't you all right? Who was that man on the street?"

She swallowed hard and paced the room, tears streaking her face as if they came all on their own. "I'm afraid I am not well at all."

"Laurel? Who was he?" her friend asked.

She brushed back the tears and turned around, though the words wouldn't come.

"Laurel, that's your husband, ain't he?" Leona's voice was soft but certain, always a good judge of character and situation.

She could only nod and force the word. "Yes."

"But you're to marry Mr. Holt, now what're ya' gonna do?" Leona whispered, panic crossing her face.

Laurel sat watching Jesse play and munch his cookie. "I don't know, Leona, but I must trust this stays with you. How could he think he can come right back into our lives? I waited for all this time, praying for his return…"

"He saying he came back for ya'?" her friend

asked.

"Yes, and that he came into his strike of gold, even showed me the deed for land in Dakota Territory where he's purchased a homestead for us. Lands, oh, Leona what am I to do?" She leaned into Leona who hugged her.

"He's a-stayin' at the hotel I'm a-reckon?" she asked. "He was walkin' that way."

"Yes, and said we can discuss things more tomorrow, that he knew I was shocked but that I was his wife and Jesse his son and he said he left a note when I thought him gone, with money for us. I don't know, maybe he did, but no one in camp could be trusted and he was earnest in his words." She shrugged. "What must I do and what will I tell him and then what will I tell Caleb?"

"Laurel, you're still married to him so you don't have much choices." Leona shook her head. "You can't marry Caleb with your husband done come back."

"I don't know, but tomorrow is Sunday and Caleb will wonder why we aren't at the ranch." Laurel shook her head. "I suppose I will make an early trip to the hotel and discuss things with Jonah, explain about Caleb and our plans, but…I am still Jonah's wife."

"I'll come and keep Jesse for ya', he ain't much trouble, but you think your husband just gonna let you go get married to Caleb?" Leona's question was sincere. "He won't be a hurtin' ya or anything if'n he finds out will he?"

"No, he was never abusive, but…Oh lands, I prayed so long for Jonah to return, never thinking he would. And I've promised Caleb a lifetime together…" She let the tears streak her face. What on earth was she to do?

"Well, you're in a fine fix of a mess, but don't you love Mr. Holt?" Leona whispered in question.

"Yes, but I once loved Jonah too, and he's Jesse's father." She kept her words low with Jesse nearby.

"Want me to stay with ya' tonight?" her friend asked.

She quickly wiped her face. "No, Leona, you've been more than gracious to listen to me and care for Jesse, I'll bring him to you come morning and I'll go to the hotel to talk with Jonah."

Leona went to the door. "I'll not say a word to no one, even the widow."

"Thank you, Leona."

Her friend went out the door, leaving Laurel who paced a bit more and then sat to play with Jesse out of sheer need to be close to him. Her heart raced, her mind wandered and she pretended to be normal for Jesse, playing and laughing as though she were fine, but inside her heart was crushed to tiny pieces.

Chapter Twelve

Laurel rose early, putting on one of her dresses and taking time with her hair and nice boots. The night before had become an endless worry where sleep had not found her, except for dozing on and off a few minutes apart. She'd taken Jesse to Leona just a bit ago and she was heading to the hotel to find Jonah, though she little knew what she was to say to him.

That Jonah was alive if nothing else, was a relief, even if he had abandoned her and Jesse. And in short there was something to the fact he had returned. All the shame she'd suffered as a woman whose husband had left wanted to fade, but maybe quick forgiveness wasn't the answer. Trusting Jonah once more would be difficult even if he was Jesse's father and her sense of duty said she was still his wife.

She'd had no way of letting Caleb know that she wouldn't be at the river this afternoon. She wasn't sure what she would say to him either. He'd done not a single thing wrong, accepting her and Jesse as his own. Jonah had said he'd come back for her and Jesse, but what if she told him she would not be going with him? He would still have rights to Jesse under the Wyoming territory laws. The thought made her shiver and she would not part with her son, ever.

And what if Jonah was sincere, her love for him hadn't simply left her mind and heart, though trusting him would be an issue. What was she to do? She supposed it wasn't impossible to love two men at the same time and both for different reasons. Why had her entire life been like this, where there was always give and take, gain and loss no matter her turns?

She had loved Jonah, or she had loved the man he'd been when she met him. She supposed that was the love of a girl, falling in love for the first time. But finding herself abandoned and alone had changed her perception of what love was supposed to mean. Caleb had picked up the pieces of her lonely heart and loved her in spite of it all. Even in his bed, she'd been free to love him as she desired. But now that love may have turned into the ultimate sin against her husband.

It was now she wished she had the advice of her mother. While her heart would always choose Caleb, Jonah was Jesse's father, not that at this point he deserved that privilege any longer. But as it was, he had come back for them both.

She glanced outside, where a light rain had begun, and lifted her bag over her shoulder and made it to the streets of Wylder, headed for the hotel, walking against the buildings to catch their covering. The town was busy and as she came into view of the hotel, she slowed her pace, took a deep breath and then climbed the few steps to the two-story structure.

Inside, her heart raced, but the memories that surfaced were difficult. Nine months before, arriving with a toddler on horseback and a sewing machine and single bag of clothing was a quick reminder of her abandonment. She'd had only a few dollars and the night clerk had turned her away from the hotel, though one of the maids had motioned her from outside and

132

allowed her the night stay in a small cot in a closet in the basement of the hotel. At the time, she didn't want to fall into the hands of trouble, but exhaustion had long taken her and Jesse had given up his squalling for sleep once she'd fed him.

Once she found the job as seamstress, she'd made sure to return the kindness and had made the girl a beautiful shawl, adding a couple of dollars to the pocket. Strange all these months later she'd never seen the woman again. But that was the thing about Wylder, people in and out of town all the time.

The hotel was lit with bright chandeliers and had velvet couches and draperies as modern and fancier than any of the buildings in Wylder and her pulse raced at entering the facility once more. The lobby was full of people visiting and couples in the restaurant having breakfast.

Scanning the lobby, she spied Jonah sitting at a table with another gentleman who wore the same fine clothing, that a bit of a shock about Jonah. Perhaps she'd come at an inconvenient time but before she could sit to wait, he spotted her, turning back to his conversation with a nod and a handshake.

Jonah walked toward her. "Morning. I was about to come find you. You didn't bring Jesse along with you?"

She shook her head. "No, Jonah, I didn't because we must talk and he would never sit still for long."

Jonah held her gaze as if he didn't understand, but then he didn't know how busy Jesse could be. "Well, perhaps we can talk in my suite."

"No, I would prefer here, not your room." Lands, a suite at a hotel would be expensive, wouldn't it?

"Of course." He nodded to where he'd been sitting

with the gentleman and led her that direction.

Laurel seated herself, the lobby full of people but no one terribly close to them. Perhaps more people were inside given the weather.

Jonah took his seat after her. "I am sorry for startling you last night. But my search has taken me so long. When I was told a woman with a small child worked at the dress shop, I assumed I might find you, and I just couldn't wait."

"Jonah…" Laurel started but he spoke once more.

"Laurel, let me explain first better than I did last night." He tried to explain.

She waited, his blue eyes studying her as he continued. "Look, I did leave a note and what money I had. About six dollars. I came back to camp and you and Jesse were sleeping and I had to decide that night to take the spot. I knew I'd hit, Laurel, but not one day did I ever not think of you both."

He shook his head. "And now I can make things how you wanted them, with a real home, say you'll go with me, and let me make things right again."

She held his gaze for a long moment. "I never thought you'd return and no matter the money or a note…Jonah, you left me. You left your son, a toddler, a baby, to the wilds of the territory without so much as a word." She forced herself to lower her tone. "Do you know how difficult it was to maneuver Pink through those mountains to this town? When I got here, I hadn't but a few coins and was turned away from this very hotel."

She fought tears and raised her voice. "I had a tired horse, a screaming child and no way to feed either and I was exhausted. And had it not been for a very kind woman, we would have spent several nights in the alleyways until I got the seamstress job."

"I'm sorry, Laurel." Thunder sounded off a ways and a harder rain began to fall. "You have to know I did so with the best intentions. What kind of man would I be that I never found a way to make a proper home for you and Jesse, had I not tried?"

"Jonah, what kind of man leaves a woman and a child like that? No matter the note or money. You were gone and I was only to assume you'd never return. And I have fought to make the money Jesse and I needed to eat and for Pink's upkeep." She took a deep breath. "I loved you Jonah, maybe part of me still does, but I've…" She hesitated in telling him of Caleb but then she had to make it known. "Jonah, I thought you would never return and I went on with my life. I've plans to be married to a local rancher."

His just looked at her. "Laurel, you're my wife."

"No, Jonah, you lost that privilege," she added, wanting to fight to make him see the truth of it.

"But Jesse is my son," he scolded, shaking his head. "And I will not part with him or you, Laurel. You must give me this chance to make things right."

"You left, Jonah…" She was surprised at her tone. "What was left for me to do but find my way and I have."

"I have the homestead waiting for us. You must come to your senses of this. You are my wife and Jesse is my son and I've returned to take you both home, to a home we'll build together." His voice was stern, maybe as harsh as he'd ever been with her.

"Jesse is my son and regardless your decisions, he is mine by the laws of the territory. And I beg you to consider this and how much I love you both." His voice was surprisingly soft, throwing her off in her own thoughts. "Laurel, you can't love another given all we've been through, all we shared."

She held his gaze, some part of her still loving him, glad he was safe, but the other part of her fully in love with Caleb.

"I wanna see Jesse and spend a bit of time with you both so you can see I'm sincere in returning for you. I deserve at least that." He waited, his voice cracking as he fought to control his emotions as he squeezed her hands. "Laurel, you can't marry someone else, I love you and I was coming back and you're my wife and Jesse's my son."

Her chest tightened but she answered him with the only right things she could think of at the moment. "You may come to my room and see Jesse later tonight, but you must remember he doesn't know you, Jonah."

He nodded, an easy smile crossing his lips. "I know and I'll come and give you the time you need to think on things."

She stood, letting go of his hand. It was the right thing wasn't it, to let him see Jesse if nothing more? How could she deny him such a right, even though she was confused? "I must get to Jesse and we'll expect you around five."

He stood along with her and once more leaned to kiss her cheek. Laurel somehow made her legs carry her from the hotel and back toward her room, brushing back tears at her predicament. How on earth would she explain things to Caleb?

Or herself.

****

Laurel bent to Jesse who shied, clinging to her leg as Jonah stepped inside, removing his top hat. Jonah bent and waited, tears in his eyes over seeing his son.

"Hi, Jesse, aren't you such a big boy?" Jesse peeked around at him and hid once more. "He's bigger than I thought."

"He is three now." She hadn't explained to Jesse this was his father and she couldn't be sure what her son remembered.

She wasn't surprised at the tenderness Jonah expressed, nor was she surprised at the tears that wanted to well in the rim of his eyes as he watched Jesse and then reached into his coat.

"Jesse, I got you a little something." He showed Jesse a small metal train engine. "It's a train that winds up and it moves."

The toddler watched as Jonah twisted the crank several times and sat the small train to the floor where it took off and gave a whistle. Jesse's eyes widened and he glanced from the toy to Jonah and spoke. "Jesse's train."

Jonah gave a smile of what Laurel thought was relief and looked from her to his son. "Yes, Jesse's train." He handed it to Jesse who with a bit of hesitation took it and held it to his chest, grasping the key turn crank.

Laurel watched, wondering at the cost of such a toy, but knowing it was brand new and most likely hadn't come cheap. Given Jonah's dress and the toy and the expense of the hotel, then there wasn't any further doubt in her mind that Jonah had found his gold strike.

"There you go, put it down and let go it and it'll roll across the floor." Jonah was on his knees offering the instruction as Jesse did what he said.

Laurel let her mind drift. Caleb would come to look for her and as it was, she hoped much later than now, when his ranch work was done. The crush of her thoughts caught her again. She fought tears, watching Jonah with Jesse. She was Jonah's wife, and this man was her son's father and suddenly the decision was no longer her own to make.

"Wow, look at her go." Jonah chanted and touched Jesse's hair as he crawled to follow the metal train.

"Watch train, Mama." Jesse wound up the toy once more and put it on the floor, clapping his hands.

"Well, that is such a nice toy for you." Laurel found her words difficult as the small engine made its whistle and took off across the floor. The sun would be down in an hour and she had four days to decide for sure the fate of her life and that of her son.

Jonah stood again as he watched Jesse play. "He's so big, talking well and…handsome, a lot of hair."

Laurel walked toward the window to look across the darkening town. "It's a very nice gift, Jonah."

He stood beside her then and held out a box. "And there's something for you as well."

Laurel looked at the dark brown wood grain box and closed her fist around the ring she wore from Caleb as Jonah lifted the lid, exposing a shiny gold ring with a clear stone.

"I always promised you a ring, something to wear for us," he whispered, his deep blue eyes holding her close as a reminder of what a tender man he'd once been with her.

Tears spilled down Laurel's cheeks and she did nothing to stave them, only reached to take Caleb's ring from her finger and slide it to her dress pocket, aware that Jonah noted her actions.

"I know that's his ring Laurel, but you're my wife, and I'm gonna spend the remainder of my life making up for what I've done to you and Jesse, I can promise you that." He stepped closer and taking the ring, put it on her finger and then drew her into his chest, wrapping both arms around her.

"It's lovely," she whispered and her choice was made out of obligation if nothing more. She was Jonah's wife and he was Jesse's father and she would not part with her son.

Jonah seemed surprised at her words. "So many things have changed, Laurel, with money we can have it all, the homestead when we get to Dakota territory and fine clothing and a place to be a family."

He nodded, holding her gaze once more. "Do you remember, Laurel, how it was together, how it was to hold each other and see our future. We can have that now, all of it."

He leaned in to kiss her, taking her mouth in a deep settling kiss, that sealed the decision that had been made for her. She reacted little, but he continued and let his hands touch her body, holding her against the hardness of his tall frame.

"I'll need time, Jonah…" She pulled back, intimacy with him almost foreign.

He nodded. "I'll give you all the time you need, Laurel, to trust me again. I'll go, but I've a man I can send to help you pack your things, yours and Jesse's."

"We have little, our clothing and my sewing machine and there's…Pink." She'd thought last night about Pink and where she would fall into this.

He nodded. "We'll have to send for Pink, the railroad doesn't go all the way to the homestead and there's no animal car until next spring for as far as the track goes."

How could she leave Pink behind?

"I can pay her upkeep here and we'll send for her come spring." Jonah offered, but his tone clearly expected her resistance.

"I'll go for now, see you come morning and help you any way you need." He kissed her again. "I want you to come willingly, Laurel, because we're a family, even Pink, later on."

Somehow, she wasn't sure she believed him but she gave a hesitant nod, having no words as her heart burst inside her chest.

Chapter Thirteen

The last of the evening sun disappeared over the horizon as Caleb urged Jericho toward the dress shop. Laurel and Jesse hadn't come to the stream or the ranch today, leaving him concerned. It had rained earlier that morning but it had tapered off by noon. He suspected Laurel was concerned about another storm given the one she'd been through. But he'd had a few horses to sell to a man who'd come to the ranch for the purchase and his work had taken him longer than he'd expected.

He dismounted from Jericho and glanced up to her room, where a dim light burned. He smiled, supposing he'd be a bit of a surprise and wanting her in his arms. He climbed the stairs and waited at her door listening and then giving a light tap.

It took a moment but the door opened, though Laurel never asked of who it was.

"Better be careful, woman, opening the door to the likes of a stranger." He chuckled and took her in his arms, kissing her, though she tensed.

"What is it?" He set her to her feet again and glanced where Jesse lay sleeping and back. Her face was red, tears streaking her cheeks. "Laurel?"

She turned away from him and after a moment spoke. "He came back, Caleb, Jonah did."

The heart inside Caleb's chest skipped a beat and a half before he could fathom what she had said. He couldn't utter a word.

"He's come back for Jesse and me." Her voice didn't waver as she held out her hand, tears still streaking her face.

He held out his own and opened his hand as she withdrew hers and there lay the ring he'd made for her, the one with the green stone that had belong to his mother. He studied the ring and then glanced back to her. "Laurel?"

She didn't give him a chance to say anything more as she continued. "Jonah came back yesterday and he's returned for us, has a homestead in the Dakota Territory he's purchased. We'll leave within the week, Thursday."

Caleb blinked hard. "So you're saying good-bye? Laurel, please…"

She said nothing.

"Laurel, he left you and Jesse in the God-forsaken wilderness alone and he waltzes back in here after a year like all is well and you accept that?" He fought not to raise his voice.

"You can't know how sorry I am, Caleb, but he's Jesse's father and as I've known, I'm still married to him. I'm a woman and our choices are few." Her brows narrowed but she looked away.

"No, Laurel, he lost that right, you owe him nothing and neither does Jesse." He wanted to reach for her, pull her to him and hold her to make her see he was right. "Men like him don't change, Laurel, and we both know that."

She turned, sniffling, and he reached out to turn her to face him again. "If you're telling me good-bye Laurel, the least you can do is face me. Now, I love you, Laurel and we can fight this, your being married can be annulled. He has no rights to you and you know it."

"He's Jesse's father and what rights do I have to change that, Caleb, in spite of my heart?"

Damn but words were difficult. It seemed she'd made her mind up to the inevitable. "Laurel, what we have, our future you can't compare to what he brought back. I love you and I love that little boy right there and he can't possibly know that kind of love given he left you both."

She held her gaze steady to him. "It's best this way Caleb, even if it's not easy for either of us. I can't take Jesse from him and I won't part with my son, even as much as I love you."

Caleb walked a small circle and turned to face her once more though he wasn't sure his legs could hold him much longer. "I'll always be here, Laurel, no matter the fight, no matter your choice, but I won't beg." He chuckled slightly as inappropriate as that was. "It's like with The Black, I won't break you, trying to keep you. Guess I'll have to love you enough to let go." He kissed her hard on the mouth and taking her hand, placed the ring back into her grip. "This was made for you." And with that he walked back outside her door, forcing himself not to look back.

****

Caleb sat at the ridge as the sun rose behind him, adding light to the valley of horses below as far as he could see. His mind was clear for the first time since he'd left Laurel in her room. He'd spent two days on a drunk, something he'd rarely ever done. He figured it was Russ who'd gotten him back to the ranch after he'd spent the first night drinking an entire bottle of bourbon and riding Jericho hard toward the drop off, only to turn the horse hard to save them both.

He glanced at Jericho, who grazed nearby oblivious and trusting as always, the horse never thinking Caleb would have run them both off. He shook his head and split a large length of grass as he sat, the day promising to be hot. He stuck the tip to his mouth, his stomach rumbling in hunger and his chest so tight he wasn't sure each next breath would come—without her.

He'd never loved as he had Laurel. He wasn't sure what the rest of his life meant at this point. She was gone, or at least she would be on the train in a few days, slipping from his grasp forever. She hadn't wanted the decision she'd made but she'd never admit that. All she could see was she was married and Jonah Adams was Jesse's father and as a woman she'd felt there was no other choice.

He'd fought to control his temper, because in loving her, he wouldn't have made her choices harder. He wouldn't have taken from her what she'd found to be the right decision for herself and her son, even if it killed him. And simply, it just might yet. He stared at the full bottle of hot bourbon on the ground beside him. A sip might ease his pounding head, but the drink might just cut all he was feeling and give him the strength to go into town and kick Jonah Adams's ass like he deserved. It wasn't likely to change anything, though. It would only make things harder on Laurel and probably prove little.

He'd seen it in her eyes, she hadn't wanted that decision but she was a woman of purpose not finding another way to be the truth of what she had to do.

Russ rode up slowly and dismounted his horse, Diablo, letting go of the reins. "Thought I might find you here. Worried about you, boy."

Caleb turned back to the view before him, having expected Russ but not. Seemed it was always Russ who'd found him here as a youngster when his father had been too hard on him, something that was common. Maybe he'd even come here expecting his uncle would show.

Russ walked over and sat, adjusting for comfort. "Been a long time since we talked here, maybe a few years."

He said nothing.

"Guess you slept it off." Russ's words were soft. "Or are ya' planning for more racing against the cliff?"

Caleb glanced at the bottle lying beside him. "Ain't decided."

Russ chuckled. "It didn't work too well for ya', leastwise you didn't ride Jericho over the edge."

Caleb looked at him. "You saw that, too?"

Russ nodded. "I's watchin'. Scared the hell right out of me but figured you'd your own demons to fight over this one."

Caleb wanted to chuckle. "Then you know that, too?"

"Didn't take much to figure the talk about the man who'd returned for his wife and son. Seems he hit the big time, gold strike in the Dakotas or thereabouts." Russ stared ahead. "Did what you had to, I reckon."

"She'd her mind made up." Caleb said it, shaking his head. "It wasn't for me to stop her, make it harder for her."

"She'll love you for that, for making it easier for her when it comes down to it." Russ added.

Caleb cursed. "Son of a bitch leaves her and a child alone in the middle of nowhere and then waltzes back in here a year later like all is well. He don't deserve either of them. Might be I aim to kick his ass once and for all. What would you know about it anyway?" Russ meant well, but he didn't need a lecture and his anger still rode the surface.

Russ leaned forward, wrapping his arms over his knees. "I know plenty of it. Lived one pretty similar to this one myself, 'cept her name was Sarah."

Caleb shot him a quick glance. Sarah was his mother and he knew some of this already, though his uncle didn't know that.

"I know this right well." Russ shook his head. "She was a beauty. I met her first ya' know, that blond hair and those pretty blue eyes, had me smitten in as much as a minute."

Caleb wasn't sure he wanted to hear more.

"Ahh, but as it was, as much as I loved her, she fell for your father. He'd started the house, had the business going and I's the one always out riding to the next herd...away long enough to lose her." He stopped, staring out across the valley spread out below them.

"And you let him have her?" Caleb finished for him. He already knew the story and he was losing himself again to the pain, glancing at the bottle of bourbon next to him.

"No!" Russ shouted, the echo filling the air and the ricochet speaking it again and again until it faded far over the western rise.

Caleb looked at him, his uncle's voice cracking, it

being rare he'd ever seen Russ near tears.

"No. I didn't let him have her. I let her have him. Even though she carried my child, because she loved him." Russ shrugged. "Sometimes the right thing is the thing that hurts the most."

Caleb's heart raced. His father had told him the same things on his deathbed, that Russ was his true father. He'd never said anything to Russ, but did as he'd been instructed by his Pa, to watch out for his uncle and keep him out of trouble. So why was Russ telling him now?

"It's true, boy, like it or not," Russ whispered. "She loved Rick and I had to love her enough to let you both go."

While it was a shock, it wasn't that in its entirety. "So I'm my father's son after all."

He chuckled. "Oh, you're a lot of him, but never told you that until now. Was no need. Rick did right by you even though he knew, too. He loved you, boy and I did too, enough to walk away."

As long as truths were being told, Caleb added the rest. "And Cane told me you'd a family, a wife and daughter, those years you were gone."

Russ nodded. "Not long after I left here. Married Audrey, a friend of mine for a time since I's young. Oh, I loved her, had us a baby girl." Russ's lips curled into a smile. "Both of 'em, the reddest hair I ever seen. And my little girl, Hannah had the biggest smile. I still hear her laugh sometimes…"

The silence hung between them for long moments. "I's out huntin', it being a hot summer, game was scarce, went farther than usual and I had a inkling of something not being right. There was a wildfire, took down near thirty homes, lost 'em both just like they slipped right from my hands, not a damn thing could've been done." Russ's voice broke slightly.

"I'm sorry for that." He glanced at his uncle, the pain almost visceral.

He shrugged then. "About the same time you lost your mother. When I got word, figured I'd done nothing but hide in a bottle, so I turned tail and came back here. Rick never said a word, put me to work like not a minute had passed. But there you were, spittin' damn image of me as a boy. And I imagine your Pa had to look at that every day of his life. But he did right by you, like I said, and all I've ever been is proud."

Caleb looked out across the sky before them. "Not even who I thought I was then?"

"Nope, you're Caleb Holt no matter, none of it changed much," his uncle…father…was quick to answer. "Just because I let her go, doesn't mean I wanted to, no more than you watching Laurel do what she must."

"She don't love him, she can't after what we…" Damn, making love to her had been life changing for him. She had to have known that, too.

In the distance, the herd with The Black ran past, stopping outside the fence line.

"Damn, there's The Black." Caleb shook his head and watched as the stallion reared and neighed to the entire valley.

"You ever thought about the reason she loves so hard? It's because she knows what it's like to be loved so little." Russ went on. "She's doing what she has to for her son, no different than me. You got an inkling to go to town to kick his ass, well, it isn't gonna end well for her or you if you do that. It's like that Black, you break her spirit, you lose her anyway, no matter you take him down a notch or not. But you let her go, if she's really yours, she'll find a way to make it so. So why don't you put that bottle away and get back to your work?"

Russ got up then and turned to walk back to Diablo.

"Russ?" Caleb didn't turn but waited.

"Huh."

"I knew I was your son, Pa told me before he died," Caleb confessed and then turned to face his father. "I was proud about it if that helps?"

Russ chuckled. "Jackass couldn't even take that secret to his grave then."

Caleb watched as the man he most admired in the world rode back toward home, leaving him to contemplate more than his mind could gather at once.

Chapter Fourteen

Laurel packed the last of her trunks. The night before had brought her little sleep with all that had happened in Jonah's return. Tomorrow the train would leave for the Dakotas and she and Jesse would leave Wylder behind for the homestead with Jonah. She'd settled up with the widow for the last of her pay, the old woman coming to tears when she'd wished her well. It was then she'd touched the wedding dress she'd started for her marriage to Caleb, but she'd turned to leave it behind there in the dress shop, not looking back.

How could she? It was perfect, the most beautiful she'd ever made, but the dream of marriage to Caleb would never happen now. Maybe her heart and the ability to love wouldn't ever be part of her again. Caleb must surely hate her.

But she had to stand by her decision as being the right thing for Jesse, no matter that her heart would be shattered for a lifetime. And not surprising, but Caleb…he'd been kind and his words forced but he'd allowed it and left her, though he'd given her back the ring he'd made for her. So why wasn't it easy? Why did it feel like the world was all but coming down right on top of her?

"Well, you 'bout got it all." Leona closed the trunk. "Not another thing will fit in this'un."

Laurel nodded, glancing at Jesse who had played

non-stop with the train Jonah had given to him. "Yes, it's all packed."

"Laurel, I'm gonna miss ya' more than anyone, even losing my Ma and Pa." Leona wiped her eyes. "It's gonna be right sad without you here."

"I know, but it's best that Jesse should know Jonah." Laurel wasn't sure if she was trying to convince her friend or herself.

"If'n you're asking me, not worth as much as how much Mr. Holt loves you both." Leona explained further. "I know you're a married lady, but this seems all wrong."

Laurel only nodded. "Sometimes, choices in life are not easy ones for a woman as I've said."

Leona nodded. "I'll watch Jesse if'n you need to take Pink."

Laurel's belly tightened, as she'd paid Pink's upkeep in full and had the horse tied outside the dress shop. She hadn't asked Caleb but as much as it would break her heart further, she had to leave Pink behind and the only place she felt the horse would be cared for was by Caleb. "Thank you, Leona. I think Pink will be happier on the ranch and I need one more chance to explain things to Caleb, and find a way to say good-bye once more."

"Break that heart of yours all over again, if ya ask me." Leona folded her arms. "I'll stay here with Jesse so he can play."

Laurel grabbed her riding hat, already wearing her riding pants and vest as if she were headed to the stream to play with Jesse once more. She turned to her son. Maybe she would miss that the most, the time she could never regain with her son—or Caleb.

151

"Jesse, play with Leona with your train, Mama won't be long." She tousled his hair, though he didn't even glance up.

She made her way outside, taking nothing with her, save the horse and herself. She hadn't planned this or asked of Caleb to keep Pink but she could only fathom he would care for the horse properly. And maybe he deserved at least a real explanation and good-bye though she wasn't sure she could manage it.

She patted Pink. Jonah had said they could send for the horse later but she couldn't see putting the animal back on a train as she had from back East. The horse hadn't traveled to it well and she'd scolded herself time and again for having insisted on bringing her west back then and it was best to leave her behind this time.

She rubbed Pink's broad face and kissed her, and there was no way to explain anything to her either. She sniffled and mounted up, taking the animal on a gallop out of town toward Caleb's ranch, hoping she'd find some kind of peace she might live with, even if she knew she'd never heal, nor would he.

Pink took to a run on the edge of town, as Laurel's tears blocked her vision and the sun pelted down across her. She slowed at the stream and more tears fell, though she dried her face as the ranch came into view. She had no idea if Caleb would be at the ranch or out to his work though. As she slowed Pink he came out of the barn and stood watching her ride the horse in.

She stopped Pink and waited a moment, pushing the hat from her head and dismounting. She didn't move closer to him at first, though he stepped to her, his face holding a blank stare as if he were playing a game of dead eye poker. Well, she needed to take her own medicine and speak first as best she could.

"I know I've no right asking you, but I won't be able to take Pink along tomorrow. I should've made arrangements with you, but she'd be happy here under your care." She bit her bottom lip to keep the tears at bay.

Caleb nodded. "She'll be fine here."

Laurel held his gaze. "We leave tomorrow on the evening train, but I felt that I should speak to you once more, that you deserved at least that."

He waited, saying nothing, though why should it be his to do?

"I have no words to make this any better for either of us." She swallowed hard, the tears coming anyway, though she brushed them away with her hand. "Caleb, be kind to yourself and…in time, allow yourself the love of another as you are deserving of it."

He still remained quiet, though his deep brown eyes showed the pain.

She turned.

"Wait, I've something for Jesse." He trotted off and returned a short time later with a small wooden cage.

Laurel glanced at it and as he got to her she realized it was Harold, the rooster inside.

"Harold's a bit lonely, made him a small cage, was gonna have Russ bring it to you tonight." He sat the cage on the ground beside him. "There's a bit of chicken feed in the bag, for the trip."

Laurel could only grin. "He's asked of Harold….and you."

He stepped closer as she offered him Pink's reins. His hand found hers as he reached for the horse and he pulled her closer instead. "Have a good life Laurel, I'll love you always."

His lips met hers and she tasted her tears mingled with his as she clung to him for a long moment, thinking she might simply die of her shattered heart.

"Good-bye, Caleb." With that she bent to pick up Harold's cage.

"I'll take you back to town, Laurel," he offered.

"No, I'd prefer to walk, please." She turned thinking she might never again take in a single breath of air where she didn't think of him.

"Then give us a minute and I'll have Russ drive you in, you can't go alone with no horse." He stopped her by touching her arm. "I insist Laurel, just a bit and I'll send Russ out."

"The I would like to wait near the stream for a moment until Russ is ready," she said.

"All right."

And as he turned, Laurel watched him enter the barn and only then did she take the path toward the stream, her vision blurred by tears she was sure would never end.

****

Caleb shoved the bottle of bourbon he'd yet to touch into his saddle bag and tied Jericho. An hour before he'd sold two mares to a man in town and as it was, Russ had mentioned that he'd seen Jonah Adams in the saloon each evening he'd been there and he was hoping that might be the same thing tonight.

He wasn't going to start any fight but he had a few things to say to the man when he came out. And it just might be in his long ride back to the ranch he'd suck down the bottle of bourbon to ease the pain he was now wearing as heavy as armor.

He'd waited a couple of hours now and on a quick peek into the saloon he'd spotted the man he thought to be Jonah Adams. A part of him wanted to tear the bastard apart but that would prove no good in his book of making things right for Laurel, but he was going to say what needed to be said to the man who taken away the woman and child he'd grown to love.

A few men left the saloon, laughing and slapping each other on the back and were followed shortly by Jonah. Caleb waited and then called to him.

"Jonah Adams?"

Jonah turned slowly, eyeing him. "Depends on who's asking?"

Caleb stepped closer, noting the man wore a gun same as he. "I'm Caleb Holt."

The man eased a hand toward his weapon.

Caleb shook his head. "Don't reach for your revolver unless you're planning to use it."

"I know who you are, Holt, and I know about you and my wife. That's right, she told me, but she's my wife and we'll be leaving town tomorrow, so you'll have no worries of her after that." Jonah narrowed his gaze, his hand still riding near his weapon.

Caleb wanted to curse. "Wrong. She is my concern, or worry as you put it, but then you can't really know how things were for her, being you left her in the middle of hell's nowhere with a child in search of your gold dust. And now you come back for her because you hit, but as I see it, rarely do men like you change."

"Look, you have no right to accuse me of anything," Jonah sparred, stepping closer.

"No? Well as I see it, I do, because men like you

155

never change, those searching for that endless pile of gold or silver or something of its like," Caleb spat.

"I plan to do right by her and my boy and it's time you moved along." Jonah tilted his hat back in further challenge.

"She deserves better than what you did to her. If I find out it happens again, won't be no law this side of hell to stop me from teaching you the lesson you deserve." Caleb shook his head.

"You know nothing of it at all," Jonah challenged.

"Tell me you're gonna be the man that she deserves, the man who stays around, not running off from one find to the other, neglecting her and Jesse. Say she'll find you to be the man she thinks you are and the father that Jesse deserves, not just here and there but every damn day, because if not, I'll hunt you down and take care of you once and for all." Caleb didn't move as Jonah lifted his revolver.

"You gonna shoot me for the truth, Mr. Adams, for the truth she knows about you, too? You don't deserve her, but she's doing what she thinks is best so don't disappoint her or I'll make it my mission to do away with you once and for all." Caleb turned back to Jericho, tasting the hurt he wanted to inflict.

"She's my wife, Holt, and it's time you let her go." Jonah Adams held the weapon poised still.

Caleb stood his ground but spoke once more. "She deserves to smile each and every day of her life, you make sure that happens for them both."

Jonah nodded, reholstered his gun and turned back toward the hotel, leaving Caleb to mount up and drive Jericho hard into the darkness.

Chapter Fifteen

Smoke from the evening train's engine filled the platform at the depot in Wylder as Laurel sat on a bench waiting for Jonah. He'd gone to send a telegram of their pending arrival outside of Deadwood where they would pick up the deed to their homestead. Beside her, Jesse sat with Harold's cage on his lap, the tiny fowl inside seemingly happy to be back with her son.

They were both dressed for the journey north and Jonah would be back any minute so they could board the train and find their seats. As it was, she'd said her good-byes once more thanking the widow for the job and her room in a time she had needed both. And she'd had to fight tears in telling Leona farewell, the younger woman crying in sniffles as she'd walked away. And yesterday, she had left Pink with Caleb finding some semblance of telling him she would always love him, though she feared all she'd done was to upset them both again.

Her life would go on as would his, but she fathomed she'd never love as she had loved him. And maybe in another life it might have been different. It was still a shock that Jonah had returned and even more of one that they were about to board the train for Dakota Territory.

She'd tried to explain the move to Jesse and that Jonah was his father, but he'd said little. She supposed he was confused by it all. How could he be expected to understand something she wasn't sure that she did? But people were beginning to board the train and Jonah had not yet returned. She stood then as Leona came running up to her once more.

"Laurel, oh thank the heaven's you're still here and haven't boarded yet." Leona grabbed her arm trying to catch her breath. "You can't go, you gotta listen to me."

"Leona, what on earth?" She steadied her friend, shaking her head.

"Laurel, the men in the saloon are all talking about it, all of 'em, even Jonah's there, you can't go, he'll just do that to you again." Leona talked so fast she could hardly understand her.

"Slow down, what of Jonah?" She held Leona's gaze.

"You can't go, the men, they're all talking about a find somewhere in Rogue River, that's Oregon ain't it? They're all a-sayin' they're heading that way and Jonah's the same, making plans for there, Laurel, he ain't truthful to you." Leona held her hands squeezing so tight she drew her hands away and back up shaking her head in disbelief.

"No, Jonah went to send a telegram about our homestead," she explained, glancing behind her, deep dread flushing through the center of her chest. Jonah wouldn't…but then she had no doubts Leona's story was true.

"No, I had to deliver a load of laundry to a man staying upstairs at the saloon, and Laurel, Jonah's in there a talking just like all those men…he ain't a-being true to you, Laurel. He's planning to go to Oregon." The wash woman and friend lowered her voice.

"Laurel, you can't leave Wylder or he'll leave you and Jesse alone once again."

Was Jonah doing just that? Being in the saloon would explain his delay, and here she waited with her son, her sewing machine, luggage and a tiny rooster in a cage. It all came to her as Jonah turned the corner with a huge smile on his face.

She turned, but Leona had disappeared.

Jesse began to cry. "Jesse go, now."

Laurel picked him up. "It's all right."

Jonah searched his coat pocket for their tickets. "Sorry, got caught up at the land office." He held the tickets up with a grin. "You ready?"

Laurel shook her head and patted Jesse who now screamed. "Want Papa, Papa."

She followed Jesse's glance to the other side of the train and caught a glimpse of Caleb waiting there and every ounce of her being knew what she had to do.

"Jonah, there's no homestead in the Dakotas, is there?" She laid it on the line for all that she knew to be true and she should have known long before now that while he was her husband, he would never change.

"Laurel, yes, there's land…" Jonah shook his head confused, his brows narrowing.

"But you have no deed. Tell me you weren't in the saloon discussing the gold find at Rogue River in Oregon." She raised her voice, pent up anger flowing to the surface. "Tell me you aren't a part of the men planning to go there, Jonah."

"Laurel,…we need to board, we can talk about this on the way." He denied nothing, though his voice rose an octave and he grabbed her arm. "There's land near Deadwood we can claim…"

"But no deed? Jonah for God's sake tell me the truth of it, now," she yelled as Jesse continued to scream for Caleb. She couldn't believe it was happening again and yet, there was no surprise to it at all. She had known this all along, even if he was admitting nothing.

"Laurel, calm yourself, it isn't what you think, yes, I was in the saloon because I've men I can put there to dig at Rogue River and yes, I'll go there, once we settle," he tried to explain, talking in a stifled whisper.

"You haven't answered my question of the deed, Jonah!" she shrieked, jerking away from his grasp, people on the depot docks stopping to watch and whisper, but she cared little.

"All right, there's no deed, Laurel, but we can claim the land once there." He reached for her again but she stepped aside, keeping Jesse tight to her, Harold's cage in his grasp.

She shook her head. "Jonah, Jesse and I aren't coming along as I have no doubts you'll leave us once more to go to that claim."

"This is about him? That rancher Holt, then?" He asked, his brows narrowing and hushed whispers filling the depot.

"No, this is about your love of gold and who you are, Jonah. Think of it like this…" She juggled Jesse to her other hip. "You're free to go right to the gold rush without having to take a woman and child, that will only weigh you down and you know it, that's why you left us before. So I'm giving you that freedom, Jonah. We're staying here in Wylder, so you won't have to lie any longer and you're free to go to your digs."

"Laurel, I love you and Jesse is my son, my son."

He shook his head, pointing a hard finger at her.

"Jonah, he doesn't even know you, not really." She held his gaze and then fighting tears told the truth of it. "He's calling for the only Pa he knows and it's not you, Jonah. It's not you."

It was a long moment before Jonah spoke. "Laurel, I never meant for this to happen, but…"

Laurel stopped him. "It's all right, Jonah, it's the best of things and we won't be in your way, you can take this train on to Oregon and never look back. And I won't live like that ever again, Jonah. It's just not meant to be for us and you know it as well as I do."

"You'll go to him then?" Jonah shook his head, turning a full circle and then stopping to hold her gaze once more.

She nodded. "Yes."

"All aboard!" The conductor waited nearby, patrons beginning to board the iron engine.

Jonah looked behind him at the waiting train and then to her again. He reached and touched Jesse's head. "I could have made it right, Laurel."

"For how long, Jonah? A few months? A year? And then what, me and this child or children alone in a cabin in the Dakotas….no, Jonah." She hugged Jesse, who sniffled.

Jonah shook his head, tried for words he never found. He offered her a slight smile and simply turned to board the train not looking back at her or Jesse.

She turned and scanned the crowd across the way for Caleb. He was no longer there. Her heart sank as if she were lost all over again in Wylder. She moved back to her bags and the heavy sewing machine in its case, sitting near the bench.

She put Jesse to his feet. "Hold on to Harold, we're going home."

Jesse gripped the tiny cage still sniffling as she tried to gather their bags.

"Funny thing about women and horses."

Laurel whirled at the sound of Caleb's voice.

"If you set them free, don't break their spirit, they come back it seems, sooner or later." He stepped closer and Jesse ran to him. "Even the ones with wild hearts."

"Papa, go home," the boy chattered as Caleb lifted him and Harold. "Harold want to go home."

Laurel swallowed hard, not wanting to allow her tears that escaped anyway. "You were right, gold was discovered in Oregon it seems."

He walked closer carrying her son. "Heard about it."

"We sent him on his way, he was going to go anyway…apparently." She tried to explain, but what was she to say to him now after all she'd done?

Caleb nodded again.

"You were right about him but I…I had thought it best, even if it nearly crushed me to tell you good-bye." She tried, though explaining was difficult.

He brushed back Jesse's hair as the wind blew it across his brow and stood him to his feet again. "Like The Black, I had to let you go so you could see for yourself. Somehow, I knew you would. But if I hadn't, then you might have carried regrets I couldn't fix."

She just held his gaze, the entire fact very true. "Seems I didn't give you much choice of it, though can you ever forgive me in thinking that the right choice?"

Caleb reached out a palm and let it rest on her cheek. "Done."

And with that he leaned to place his lips to hers and Laurel clung to him, holding on to forever as tightly as she could and falling into his wanting embrace.

Epilogue

The early spring wind blew a chill through the barn as Caleb lifted Jesse from his shoulders and stepped to the porch. He'd been at idle work for most of the day now trying to bide the time.

"Ain't heard a thang, yet, she's keeping Coyote a-hoppin' and you're pacing again." Russ chuckled as Jesse climbed the stairs, Harold, the rooster following him up as usual.

"Well, hello there, Harold, you been busy this afternoon helping Jesse and Papa?" Russ made small talk with Jesse as Caleb slowly went out of his mind.

Laurel had gone into labor early morning and she apparently was still at it. He'd sent Cade to retrieve Doctor Sullivan, who'd arrived shortly after, along with Leona from the dress shop, both disappearing inside. The wash woman had only come out at noon to let them know Laurel was doing fine but it was taking a bit of time.

Jesse bent to the rooster and handed him a cracker. "Harold helping me sweep the barn for Papa."

"Well, roosters are good for that kind of thing." Russ chuckled as Jesse went back down the stairs and the rooster followed, clucking and pecking for gravel.

"Ahh, quit your pacing, these things can take time," his father spoke to him though he grinned.

Caleb shook his head. "She said it didn't take much

164

with Jesse, this here's a bit long I think."

Russ nodded, "Just like them horses there, when foaling, ever one of those births are different."

Caleb began to speak but stopped short as a baby's squall reached them. He turned facing the door and tilted his hat back waiting. "Come, Jesse."

The boy trotted up the steps again followed by Harold. After a long wait, Doc Sullivan came to the door, smiling.

"She all right, Doc?" Caleb's mouth was so dry it might be it was full of cotton.

Coyote nodded. "She's fine. She did well."

"The baby?" Caleb asked, his heart in his throat.

"Go on, Papa, she'll tell you about it." Coyote held the door as Caleb picked up Jesse and made his way inside and down the long hallway.

Relief that Laurel was all right was one thing, but turning the corner to enter their bedroom nearly took his breath. Before him, Laurel sat up in bed, her hair down and braided across her shoulder. And she held not one, but two bundles.

Leona smiled and made her way from the room. "I'll be back in a bit. Congratulations, Mr. Holt."

Caleb sat Jesse to his feet, the boy in as much awe as himself. He stepped closer, holding Laurel's gaze, thinking maybe he was seeing double.

"Mama got a baby?" Jesse ran to the side of the bed.

"Come on over, both of you." Laurel nodded toward the babies. "Two babies, Jesse. You're a big brother now."

Caleb stepped beside her and touched her hair, his heart so full he wasn't sure he could speak. "Twins?"

Laurel nodded to each baby. "Well, you said you'd be needing a passel of boys to run this ranch one day and let's just say we've a good start."

Caleb smiled, strange that he was fighting tears. "Boys?"

"Even Doc Sullivan was surprised, though he had told me he suspected two heartbeats on his last visit. I was simply hoping the second was my own." She eased one of the babies to him. "Here…Papa."

She handed him the first of his new sons. "I suppose this one will be Richard, and this one," she showed the baby to Jesse, "is Russell."

Jesse frowned. "Why'd you got two babies, Mama?"

"Twins happen sometimes, and now you have two brothers, Jesse." She touched her son's hair.

"Mama's hurt?" Jesse backed up, eyeing her.

"No, Mama's well, but having a baby is hard work, much less two." She looked back at Caleb as he sat and she handed off the second baby, allowing him to hold both. "I suppose I'm going to need a good bit of help coming up."

Caleb compared the little faces. "Russ will gloat of course, how we gonna tell them apart?"

Laurel looked from one new son to the other, both sleeping. "Well, Doc gave us a start." She lifted Russ's tiny foot from the blanket and a small strap of leather was tied around the eldest's of the twins ankle.

Caleb shook his head, his heart so full he thought it might explode in happiness. "Are you all right?"

"I will be, but what I'd like is rest and with the babies out, to have my body back again." She leaned into him. "I knew something was different but I just didn't think of it being two. They look like you, both of 'em."

"I told you both I'd heard two heartbeats but only the once," Doc Coyote entered with Russ following.

Russ came closer, looking over Caleb's shoulders. "Two, oughta keep you both busy for a good while. Handsome fellas."

Caleb began. "We decided already…this one here's Richard, and here, take this one, your namesake, Russell."

Russ looked from him to Laurel and back, taking the bundle and holding the infant to his chest.

"I think that's the first time I've ever seen the man speechless." Coyote grabbed his jacket and lifted his black bag. "I'll be back to check on you all tomorrow morning. Laurel, rest, let these men do the work in taking care of you and the children."

"Not speechless but honored, I reckon." Russ beamed.

"I've had two fathers all along and so I suppose it's fittin' to have a son for each. Make you a grandpa again." Caleb held his father's gaze.

Russ chuckled as the baby he held began to fuss. He was quick to hand the bundle back to Laurel. "Well, as it is, Gramps has a bit of work to do and me and this boy and the rooster are gonna leave you folks to yourselves." He picked Jesse up and shook his head. "Two, lands sakes, ain't gonna be a bit of sleep around here for a while."

Caleb watched as Russ carried Jesse back outside the room, Harold the rooster following. He turned back to Laurel who gave him a tired smile.

"I suppose we'll have our hands full, be up all

night at times," she whispered.

"I'll be right here, taking orders, ma'am." Caleb nodded. "Don't know much about babies, gonna need a good teacher I suppose."

She took the baby she held to her breast. "You'll do just fine Papa, they let you know what they need mostly."

Caleb watched her as she then took the baby he held and did the same. "Gods, you're the most beautiful woman I've ever seen Laurel, damn brave and…I love you."

"How much I love you Caleb, now and forever." She accepted the kiss as he settled in close beside her.

He watched her feed their sons, amazed at her confidence and what they'd created together. "Wish I'd known way earlier to ride up to the creek and maybe I'd have met you that whole winter before last."

"We've our whole lives, Caleb, but there is one thing I'd like in the future." She leaned into him. "The far future."

He looked at her waiting, placing a palm to one of the tiny heads.

"A daughter." She grinned.

"Well, now, I believe that might just be a promise I can keep." He kissed the top of her head and rested an arm across her and the tiny boys. "Three sons…and one woman I plan to hold the rest of my life."

"Yes, and never let me go, Caleb Holt." She closed her eyes and leaned into him.

"Not a chance," he whispered.

A word about the author...

Kim Turner writes western historical and contemporary western romance, discovering her passion of writing at the age of eight. Working as a registered nurse for over thirty years, she enjoys studying the medical treatments of the Old West as well as keeping up with the latest western movies and television series.

While she loves reading anything from highlanders to pirates, she claims to have an unquenchable thirst for the American Cowboy when choosing her reads.

Kim lives south of Atlanta with her husband and calls her greatest accomplishment the birth of one daughter and the adoption of another from China, neither of which came easy.

Kim's Motto: It's All About A Cowboy and the Woman He Loves...find Kim at:

kimturnerwrites.com

and

kimturnerwrites.blogspot.com.